SINS OF THE CHILD

Also by J. Robert Kennedy

James Acton Thrillers

The Protocol
Brass Monkey
Broken Dove
The Templar's Relic
Flags of Sin
The Arab Fall
The Circle of Eight
The Venice Code
Pompeii's Ghosts

Amazon Burning
The Riddle
Blood Relics
Sins of the Titanic
Saint Peter's Soldiers
The Thirteenth Legion
Raging Sun
Wages of Sin
Wrath of the Gods
The Templar's Revenge

The Nazi's Engineer
Atlantis Lost
The Cylon Curse
The Viking Deception
Keepers of the Lost Ark
The Tomb of Genghis Khan
The Manila Deception
The Fourth Bible
Embassy of the Empire

Special Agent Dylan Kane Thrillers

Rogue Operator
Containment Failure
Cold Warriors

Death to America
Black Widow
The Agenda

Retribution
State Sanctioned
Extraordinary Rendition

Templar Detective Thrillers

The Templar Detective
The Parisian Adulteress

The Sergeant's Secret
The Unholy Exorcist

The Code Breaker
The Black Scourge

Kriminalinspektor Wolfgang Vogel Mysteries

The Colonel's Wife

Sins of the Child

Delta Force Unleashed Thrillers

Payback
Infidels

The Lazarus Moment
Kill Chain

Forgotten

Detective Shakespeare Mysteries

Depraved Difference

Tick Tock

The Redeemer

Zander Varga, Vampire Detective

The Turned

SINS OF THE CHILD

J. ROBERT KENNEDY

Copyright © 2020 J. Robert Kennedy

This is a work of fiction. Names, characters, places, and incidents are products of the author's imagination. Any resemblance to actual persons, living or dead, is entirely coincidental.

ISBN: 9781998005383

First Edition

10 9 8 7 6 5 4 3 2 1

For the victims of the Lebensborn project.

SINS OF THE CHILD

"Freedom is when one hears the bell at seven o'clock in the morning and knows it is the milkman and not the Gestapo."

George Bidault

"It is particularly pleasing to us men in the new government that families with many children are given particular attention, since we want to rescue the nation from decline. The importance of family cannot be overestimated."

Joseph Goebbels, Nazi Minister of Propaganda
March 18, 1933

AUTHOR'S NOTE

While German ranks are given for each soldier or police officer initially, their Allied equivalent is then used. For example, *Unterscharführer* is meaningless to most people, however corporal is universally understood. This is done for the sake of clarity so you, the reader, can enjoy the book without trying to determine if an *Unterscharführer* outranks a *Standartenführer*.

PREFACE

In Nazi Germany, position meant power. The higher the position, the greater the power, the greater the wealth. Those who were in the Party from the early days were rewarded for their loyalty, receiving plum appointments, often with no qualifications. As in any totalitarian state where patronage and nepotism were a way of life, an administration was built to vet these appointments to avoid embarrassment to the Führer and his senior ministers.

But Nazis were fickle creatures, and one's good fortune could quickly turn, leaving one ostracized from the Party, and the privileges only it could provide. For those thrust into positions they could never have imagined, and the wealth this offered, it could mean losing everything, and a return to poverty or even death.

Yet the wealthy were insulated. The Nazis needed them as much as any society did, and for some of the nouveau riche, their only hope of security was through their children.

And the hope they would marry into wealth, and protect all their parents had gained through the horrors that were the reality of Nazi Germany.

Dettman Residence

Berlin, Nazi Germany

1941

Annie Dettman's heart hammered as she pressed her back against the wall, peering around the corner. The door to a section of the house she rarely went into was only feet away. Under normal circumstances, getting caught would be of no concern—the act of going through that door wasn't something about which her parents would care. But to cross that threshold into the servants' wing for the purpose she intended, would undoubtedly get her knuckles rapped should she be caught.

And if they found out the purpose of her foray, she didn't know what her parents might do.

To say they would be disappointed would be an understatement. They had such plans for her future, that if they discovered she didn't share in their dreams, they would be enraged.

Her father was a Nazi, which wasn't saying much these days, for so many were, but he had been there almost from the beginning. He was very proud of that fact, even having sat with the true senior members such as Hitler, Himmler, Goebbels, and Göring. At least according to her father. If one heard her mother speak, one would think her husband ran the Reich, and was single-handedly winning the war.

Yet her father did have power. He held sway over the futures of so many people. For years, she had tuned out most of the conversations, but it was impossible to ignore them, and she knew enough to know her father was responsible for vetting potential appointees. If someone had done you a favor, and you wanted to reward them with a job, it was her father's department that would make sure that potential candidate was worthy, and in today's Germany, that had nothing to do with qualifications, and everything to do with purity and loyalty. The lifestyle they now enjoyed thanks to her father's position, was far beyond anything they had experienced in their hometown of Munich before the accident that had immediately preceded her family moving to Berlin, and her father starting his new job.

She shuddered, her chest aching at the memory. They had moved to Berlin within days, leaving everything and everyone she had ever known behind, and it had left her lonely. Terribly lonely. Her father's position meant associating with a different type of person. Every child her age she now met were raised by true Nazis, filled with so much anger, hate, and pride, that she found it impossible to relate.

Her father had been a Nazi from the beginning, yet her impression was that he had recognized an opportunity as opposed to an ideology he could embrace. Her mother had always been a simple woman, content to clean the homes of those that could afford such a thing, but she had changed so much. In the six years since they had been here, she was almost unrecognizable. She was obsessed with being invited to the right parties and having the right people over for tea. It was so disappointing.

Then there were their plans for her that had begun from the moment she turned sixteen. When she had discovered what they were up to, she had vowed never to let them accomplish their goals, though it wasn't until six months ago that she had found a way to perhaps thwart their plans.

And tonight would be the fruition of everything toward which she had been working.

But only if she hurried. She had left work at her lunch break, and there was no time to waste before her shift resumed. She darted for the door, twisting the knob and pushing open the entrance into the servants' wing. She stepped inside, closing the door behind her, then listened. She could hear chatter coming from the end of the hall where the staff was collected for their midday meal. She rushed forward and ducked into the pantry, filling the bag gripped in her hand with the necessities she would require for tonight, including various cheeses, pâtés, and crackers.

Her eyes brightened at the sight of grapes.

She was careful not to take too much, for she didn't want anything missed. She descended the stairs to her left, into the wine cellar, and grabbed the first bottle she could reach. She knew nothing of wines, and had no idea whether what she had selected was worthy of consumption or reverence, but it didn't matter.

Her plans tonight demanded she be relaxed, at ease.

For tonight she was giving herself to a man for the first time.

Tonight, she was giving herself to the only man she had ever loved.

And tonight, she would ruin the plans her mother and father had for her.

Forever.

Charlottenstraße, Berlin, Nazi Germany

18 Hours Later

The aftermath still haunted him. The only person he had ever loved was dead, murdered, yet the confusion over what had happened, the shock of last night's events, had him almost convinced it perhaps was all a dream.

For what had unfolded was unfathomable.

As the ultimate sin had been committed, it was as if he were frozen in fear, much like he had seen in the movies, his disembodied soul witness to a crime he couldn't believe was being committed, as if he just stood there while Nosferatu claimed another desperate innocent.

Yet there was no doubt she was dead. He had watched, as if detached from his own person as the knife slit through her throat, then the furious rage that had stabbed his poor love repeatedly.

Why hadn't he stopped what was happening? Why hadn't he saved her life? Bile filled his mouth as guilt overwhelmed him at what he had done. He would burn in Hell for eternity, of that he was certain. He had run like the coward he was, and now had no clue what he should do. He couldn't go home. He should turn himself in to the police and let justice prevail, yet that wasn't what would happen in today's Germany, for more was at risk than just his life. Last night, he had destroyed one family through his actions, and if he turned himself in, his own family would be as well.

He pulled at his hair from across the street as the first police officers arrived at the scene, then scurried away through the alley he had concealed himself in since he had found the courage to return. He prayed to God for guidance on what he should do, knowing that none would be forthcoming, for he was as guilty as any in the murder of a poor, innocent woman.

A woman who had trusted him with her most precious gift.

Charlottenstraße, Berlin, Nazi Germany

"So, what do you think?"

"I think she's dead."

Kriminalinspektor Wolfgang Vogel eyed his much younger partner, *Kriminalassistent* Otto Stadler. "If you intend to be investigating homicides, I think you're going to need to be a little more thorough than that in your reports."

Stadler's cheeks flushed, unaccustomed to being challenged, his father well-connected within the Nazi Party. While Vogel was careful what he said around the young man, he was not about to let him off easy. Stadler wasn't qualified for the job. He hadn't put in the time, and was only his partner through nepotism. But that was the way things were today in Nazi Germany—one had to be a member of the Party to advance, and even then, it was who one knew, not what one knew.

As a member of the *Kriminalpolizei*, Criminal Police, Vogel was forced to be a member of the Nazi Party, as all *Kripo* were. If one refused, one lost one's job, or worse, one's life. He had a wife and two children to worry about, and had swallowed his pride taking the oath. He didn't attend any of the rallies, he didn't support the Party in any way, yet he had to live in this new reality.

And that meant biting one's tongue no matter how desperately one wanted to speak out against what was happening.

The masses had swallowed what Hitler and his ilk were spreading, and he could understand why. In the beginning, even he had to acknowledge the fact that things were better under the Nazis than they had been. Germany's loss in the *Weltkrieg*, the World War, had been humiliating, with the Treaty of Versailles debilitating. The war reparations forced upon them had bankrupted the country, and that, coupled with the Great Depression, had left most in poverty, too many starving, not knowing when or from where their next meal would come.

Hitler had offered them an alternative. He had promised to restore German pride and strength by ridding themselves of the burden of the Treaty of Versailles. It had attracted enough votes that what was once a fringe party, became a significant minority party. And then, through orchestrated events, Hitler had manipulated the Reichstag into naming him chancellor. The moment he had the power, despite never having the majority of the electorate, he had rid himself of the nuisance of elections, becoming the dictator of a nearly-failed state. But today, eight years later, Germany had one of the most powerful militaries in the world, and had conquered a significant portion of Europe.

Part of him was proud of what his country had achieved in rebuilding itself, but he had no interest in territorial conquests. Germany should have remained within its borders and insisted it be part of the global community. Instead, Hitler had taken it too far, and now that the Allies were regrouping, it was feeling the pain of war.

Reichsmarschall Göring had promised not a single allied bomber would ever reach Berlin, yet that vow had proven impossible to keep as the Allies were now regularly bombing the capital city Vogel called home. People were dying, and dying needlessly, but from his point of view, as a homicide detective, those who died during bombing raids were none of his concern, for murderers still murdered.

And judging by the sight that lay before him, they had a particularly vicious one with which to contend.

He pointed at the victim lying on the bed, the woman's naked body mutilated, her hands and feet bound with the sheets. "Tell me what you see."

Stadler became serious, recognizing he was being tested. Vogel felt for the young man sometimes. If his father weren't a senior member of the Party, he would have entered the police force at the bottom, and received the proper training to work his way up. But instead, he had been thrust into his current position years ahead of when he should have been, by a father who didn't want his son on the front. "Well, obviously it's a woman. Looks like she's late teens, maybe early twenties, blond." He reached over and opened one of her eyes. "Blue-eyed." Stadler glanced over his shoulder at Vogel. "She's a good Aryan specimen."

"She *was* a good Aryan specimen."

Stadler frowned. "Yes, you're right, of course. Sorry."

"What else can you tell me about her?"

Stadler carefully examined the body then shrugged. "I don't know. It looks like she might have been raped and then her throat was slit. And she was stabbed multiple times."

"And that's it?"

"Yes."

"Was she a prostitute? Was she a student? Did she come from a rich family or a poor family?"

Stadler eyed him. "How the hell would I be able to tell that?"

Vogel stepped forward. He pointed at her toenails, carefully clipped and painted, then her fingernails, also cut short and painted. "What do her nails tell you?"

Stadler shrugged. "She takes care of herself?"

"Yes. But her nails are clipped short. Why?"

His inexperienced partner stared at her for a moment. "She works a menial job?"

"Quite possibly. What about the nail polish? What does that tell you?"

Stadler sighed heavily. "That she's *not* a menial laborer?"

Vogel chuckled. "Quite possibly. But who can afford such luxuries these days?"

Stadler shrugged. "The rich?"

"Yes, that's a definite possibility."

"But then she wouldn't be a menial laborer." Stadler's eyes shot wide. "She could still be a prostitute, though."

"Why's that?"

"Perhaps she had a rich client who gave her the nail polish."

Vogel smiled slightly. "That's the first intelligent thing I've heard come out of your mouth today."

Stadler grinned. "Thank you." The grin was quickly replaced with a frown as he realized he had just been insulted. "Hey!"

Vogel ignored him. "That being said, it's my experience that most prostitutes keep their nails long, regardless of whether they're painted." He leaned over the body. "Her hair is tidy and styled. She has fresh makeup, no bruising or evidence of any type of perimortem injuries beyond those that occurred just prior to the assault. I can't rule out that she wasn't a prostitute, though my gut tells me she wasn't. What do the wounds tell you?"

Stadler stared at the slit throat and the numerous stab wounds to the chest and abdomen. "Whoever did this was angry?"

Vogel nodded. "That's what I was thinking as well, though I'm not so sure. It would appear that her throat was slit, then she was stabbed multiple times."

"How can you tell which came first?"

"The blood spatter. The throat was slit, cutting the artery, and that's what caused these splashes" He indicated the spray on the sheets and headboard. "Then you have a large amount of blood here." He indicated the heavy bloodstains on the sheets near her neck. "Then you have the stab wounds to the torso, where there's almost no blood. Her heart had stopped beating when these were made."

"But wouldn't that mean he waited at least a minute or two?"

"Exactly. The question is, why? She was already dead. This part of the attack was postmortem and served no purpose beyond the emotional. Whoever did this, raped her, slit her throat, watched her die, then in a fit of rage, or some other emotion, stabbed her at least a dozen times."

"A crime of passion?"

"The second part of the attack would certainly suggest something like that. It's the first part that doesn't. Slitting someone's throat and watching them die suggests to me a methodical, cold-blooded killer."

"So, someone rapes a woman, slits her throat, watches her die, then stabs her repeatedly, then leaves, taking her clothes with him."

"What's that?"

Stadler looked about the room. "I don't see her clothes anywhere."

Vogel confirmed his underling's finding. "You're right. And I don't see her purse either. Whoever did this, didn't want us to be able to identify her easily."

"What do you think that means?"

"I think it means he knew her."

"What makes you say that?"

"If this were random, and for example, she were a prostitute, murdered by a client, then he wouldn't care if she were identified, because there'd be no way to link him to her. But if he knew her, then he'd be scared we'd be able to connect him to her, so he'd want to make it as difficult as he could for us to identify her."

"But he has to know that we would eventually figure it out, wouldn't he?"

"Yes, but the longer it takes, the longer he has to destroy any evidence, establish an alibi, or just disappear."

"Where's the knife?" asked Stadler.

Vogel again examined the room. "He must have taken it with him."

"Would he do that for the same reason? Maybe it was identifiable? If he left the knife behind, we might be able to link it back to him?"

"Possibly. Though only a fool brings an identifiable weapon to commit murder."

"Crime of passion again?"

"Possible."

Stadler stared at the body. "But if he brought a knife with him, wouldn't that suggest this was premeditated?"

"It would, though a lot of people carry knives on a regular basis."

"Who? The kind of person who avails himself of the services of a prostitute?"

"Perhaps, however, again, if she were a prostitute, why try to hide her identity by taking her purse?"

"Perhaps he was just a thief."

"A thief doesn't tie up somebody, sexually assault them, then murder them in such a deliberate fashion."

Stadler threw up his hands. "Then I don't know what the hell is going on here. I don't know how anybody could know."

Vogel frowned at him. "You still don't get it, do you?"

"What?"

"Homicides aren't easy. Do you expect to walk into a scene and have all the answers handed to you on a silver platter? That's not the way it works. There are clues here. Those clues lead to questions, then we investigate and attempt to find answers to those questions, and to the questions that will follow from those. A young woman died here today. It's our job to find out who she is and who killed her, and I intend to do just that, because someone who commits a brutal murder like this is likely to do it again."

Berlin-Mitte Morgue

Hannoversche Straße, Berlin, Nazi Germany

Medical Examiner Hans Naumann looked up from the autopsy table as Kriminalinspektor Vogel entered with his Nazi loyalist partner, Otto Stadler. "Wolfgang, how the hell are you?"

"Better than she is," said Vogel, staring at this morning's murder victim. "What can you tell me?"

"Well, she wasn't raped."

Both Vogel and Stadler echoed their surprise. "What?"

"In my professional opinion, she wasn't raped."

"But she was tied up and naked!" protested Stadler. "How could you possibly say she wasn't raped?"

"All evidence suggests she had consensual sex using a condom, and that everything else that happened occurred after the sexual act was completed."

Vogel's eyebrows rose. "A condom?"

"That's illegal!" exclaimed Stadler.

Vogel wagged a finger. "Not if whoever she had sex with was a soldier."

Stadler frowned. "I can't believe one of our soldiers would be capable of such a thing."

Vogel rolled his eyes. "You can't imagine a soldier could have sex with a beautiful woman?"

"Huh?" Stadler stared at him, then his jaw dropped. "I meant murder!"

Naumann grunted. "Well, boy, you need to be much more precise in your observations if you expect to be a detective."

Vogel yanked them back on track. "Any evidence that she was a prostitute? Any STDs?"

"No, no sexually transmitted diseases."

Stadler stepped closer, staring at the body in the cold light of the morgue. He pointed at her genitalia. "But what about the blood? Doesn't that suggest rape?"

Naumann shook his head, frowning. "I'm afraid not. It appears it was her first time."

Vogel's shoulders slumped with the news. "Then she's definitely not a prostitute."

"No."

"So then, what we're saying is that this young woman had sexual intercourse for the first time, then was murdered after this consensual act?"

"Exactly. Which means she likely knew her attacker."

Vogel shook his head. "That assumes they're one and the same."

Naumann eyed him. "What do you mean?"

"Well, it's possible she had sex with someone she knew, then someone else committed the murder."

Stadler leaned against a nearby cabinet. "Then what happened to her lover? Wouldn't there have at least been evidence of a struggle?"

"He might have left and then the murderer arrived after," said Vogel.

Naumann shook his head. "Nonsense. You don't make love to a woman for her first time and then just walk out of the room, leaving her naked."

"We don't know that she was naked when he left. She might have got dressed and then the murderer came in, ordered her to take her clothes off, then tied her up."

Again, Naumann shook his head. "Talk to your wife and she'll tell you how nonsensical that is."

Vogel stared at him. "What do you mean?"

"I mean, there's not a young woman anywhere who isn't going to clean herself up after having sex for the first time before putting her clothes back on. All evidence from the photos I looked at of the scene, and from the body itself, is that she hadn't had a chance to clean up. The sex act had just been performed, and she hadn't yet got out of the bed. Whoever made love to her is almost definitely the killer."

Vogel frowned, eying the area in question. "I suppose you're right." He stared at her face. "Just who are you, and who was it that you trusted enough to lay with for the first time that would then so brutally murder you?" He sighed heavily. "These are the cases I hate the most, next to murdered children. No one should die this young and in such a horrible fashion. I can't imagine being butchered by someone I thought cared for me."

Naumann agreed. "It is tragic."

Vogel turned to leave. "Let me know if you find anything. I'll be canvassing the area.

"Will do."

Vogel left with his partner, and Naumann stared down at the lifeless face of what was once a stunning young woman. "Let's see if you have any secrets to reveal, shall we?"

Charlottenstraße, Berlin, Nazi Germany

"What's the meaning of this?"

Vogel glanced over his shoulder to find a young woman standing in the doorway of the apartment in which their victim had been murdered. He turned to face her and produced his identification. "Kriminalinspektor Vogel, Kriminalpolizei. And you are?"

The woman's face paled the moment official ID with a Nazi emblem was produced. "I'm-I'm Emilia Schmitt. Why are you here? Was there a break-in while I was away?" She immediately became concerned and rushed inside, her head on a swivel as she examined her apartment.

"No, nothing like that." Vogel pointed to a chair. "Please, sit down."

The woman sat, clutching her purse in her lap. "If there wasn't a break-in, then why are you here?"

"Is this your apartment?"

"Yes."

"How long have you been away?"

"A week. To see my parents in Frankfurt."

"And do you have a roommate?"

She shook her head. "No, it's just me."

"Did you have any friends staying here?"

"No, no one. Why? Why are you asking these questions?"

"So, no one would have any reason to be in this apartment besides yourself?"

"No, no one. What's going on. You're scaring me."

"Miss Schmitt, I'm afraid there's been an unsettling incident here. A young woman was found murdered in your bedroom this morning."

A short cry was stifled with a hand over her mouth. "Murdered? In my bedroom? Who was it?"

"We don't know." Vogel motioned to his partner and Stadler showed her a photo of the woman. "Do you recognize her?"

Emilia glanced at the photo then quickly turned away, closing her eyes before taking a deep breath, steeling for a proper look. She opened her eyes and stared. Vogel watched her as she examined the photograph, her body language indicating she was still uncomfortable. Every reaction from her so far told him she had no involvement in this murder. Whoever had slaughtered their victim wouldn't cringe at a photograph of their handiwork unless it had been a crime of passion, which he was confident it wasn't. She finally looked away, shaking her head firmly. "I'm sorry, I don't know her."

"You're sure?"

"Yes, though I have to admit, there is something familiar about her, as if I've seen her somewhere before."

"I thought you just said you didn't know her?"

"I don't. I mean, I don't know her personally. She's not one of my friends or a neighbor, or anybody that I think I deal with regularly. The face just looks familiar somehow. Maybe she just reminds me of someone, or maybe I saw her on the street one day. I just have this feeling I've seen her before."

Vogel nodded, unsure of what to make of what Emilia was saying. Too often, witnesses tried to be helpful and ended up being anything but. Part of her might think that by suggesting the woman was familiar, it might help them in the investigation. And unfortunately, because she had said what she did, he had to take it into account. Was the victim a part of her circle of friends, a friend of a friend, or an even more distant relationship, as opposed to some random stranger? If there were some connection, it might suggest how their victim had wound up here.

This was an apartment, not a hotel room, not some abandoned warehouse. Somebody lived here on a regular basis, and it had been vacant for only a week. Someone had to have known Emilia was away, and that the apartment would be empty. That suggested a connection to her. It could very well be that the victim was an acquaintance of someone Emilia knew. She might have seen the victim in a photograph or at a party somewhere, at some point in the past. The more he thought about it, the more he realized he shouldn't dismiss her observation.

"Who knew you were going to be away?"

She shrugged. "I don't know, it wasn't a secret. My friends, my family, my coworkers."

"Does anyone have a key?"

"My friend Petra does. Petra Berkner. I gave her a copy just in case I got locked out."

"Does she live nearby?"

She pointed up. "She lives right above me."

Vogel exchanged a glance with Stadler, but before acting on this new bit of information, he motioned at the room in which they sat. "Do you see anything missing?"

She shook her head. "No, nothing."

"Anything that's been moved, disturbed in any way?"

Again, a shake of the head. "No."

"Take a moment and look through the rest of your apartment. Let us know if anything, no matter how insignificant, is missing or out of place. I have to warn you, though, that the bedroom is quite disturbing."

"Yes, sir." She rose and headed directly for the bedroom. Vogel indicated for Stadler to follow her, just in case she wasn't so innocent and attempted to remove a piece of incriminating evidence.

He scribbled down several notes and glanced up from his pad as Emilia and Stadler stepped out of the bedroom and walked down the hallway to the bathroom and then the kitchen of the one-bedroom apartment. After a few minutes, they made their way back into the main living area.

"Well?" he asked.

She shrugged. "Everything looks exactly the way I left it, except for the bedroom, of course."

Vogel headed down the hallway to the kitchen, beckoning her to follow. He opened one of the cupboards he had searched earlier, where the young woman kept her glasses. "Do you see anything unusual here?"

She gasped. "I didn't think to look inside the cupboards!"

Stadler eyed them, puzzled. "What? What am I missing?"

She pointed at two wine glasses that sat upside down in the cupboard, every other glass upright. "The two wine glasses are upside down."

"So what? You didn't do that?"

"No, of course not. Everyone knows that if you put your glasses face down, they end up stinking over time. My mother taught me always to put my glasses upright so they could air out."

"And you're sure you didn't do this by accident, perhaps a lapse?" asked Vogel.

She vigorously shook her head. "Absolutely not, I would never do that. And besides, I would have had to do it twice because I can't remember the last time I had a glass of wine, let alone a glass of wine with someone else."

Vogel pursed his lips at the implications. It suggested that whoever had been in the apartment had enjoyed a glass of wine with someone else, and that was likely the murderer and his victim. It matched up with what Medical Examiner Naumann had said.

The sex was consensual.

"It would seem someone had a romantic interlude in your apartment while you were away."

Her jaw dropped and her eyes shot wide. "But who would do such a thing? What kind of person would do that?"

Stadler grunted. "Someone who would then murder their companion."

Her face slackened. "Yeah, I suppose so."

Vogel examined the kitchen. "Where do you keep your wine?"

Emilia laughed. "You do realize there's a war on, right? Every pfennig I have goes to just surviving. Like I said, I can't remember the last time I had a glass of wine, let alone a bottle."

"Then it would have had to have been brought here."

She shrugged. "I suppose. They certainly didn't get it from me."

Vogel turned to Stadler. "Have them check for any wine bottles. We might be able to get fingerprints off them."

"Yes, sir." Stadler left the kitchen to pass the orders on to the police officers outside.

Vogel pointed at the cupboard drawers. "Are you missing any knives?"

Emilia shuddered. "You think they used one of mine?"

"The knife wasn't recovered, so anything is possible."

She checked the cutlery drawer and knife block then shook her head. "Nothing seems to be missing." She pointed at the block. "Those are the only sharp ones I have. Maybe they washed it like the glasses?"

"I'll have them taken to the lab. Check the other cupboards everywhere in the house, anywhere you didn't look, and let me know if anything else is missing or disturbed."

She nodded and quickly began a more thorough search. He casually followed her, no longer concerned she was involved. Her search came up empty and she rubbed her arms, shivering. "The only thing besides the bedroom that I see out of place are those two wine glasses."

They returned to the living room and she sat in a chair by the window. "I just can't believe this is happening. What am I supposed to do now?"

"We're going to take the sheets as evidence, and we'll be back to examine everything closer. Once we're done, you'll be able to clean everything up and get back on with your life."

She shuddered. "I can't go back into that bedroom. I can't live here anymore."

Vogel felt for the young woman. Despite being accustomed to seeing death far too frequently, even he wasn't sure if he could continue living in his apartment if somebody were murdered there, even if they were a stranger. "Do you have somewhere you could stay?"

She shrugged. "I can stay with Petra upstairs for a few days, I suppose."

Vogel nodded. "I think that's for the best. We have several cleaners on file that specialize in this type of thing. We can put you in touch with one. It'll cost you some money, but it'll be far cheaper than changing apartments."

She wrung her hands, staring at the floor. "Thank you. I guess I'll have to figure out a way to pay, because there's no way I can do it myself. And you're right, there's no way I can afford to try to find another place." Her shoulders slumped. "I guess I'm going to have to learn to live with this."

"It'll get easier in time. I suggest investing in a new mattress and bed linens, some scented candles, and you'll be fine in time." He held a hand out toward the door as Stadler returned. "Now, let's go talk to your friend and see if she gave your key to anyone."

She rose and they all headed upstairs. Emilia knocked on one of the apartment doors and it was answered moments later.

"Emilia, so good to see you! When did you get back?" The woman's pleased expression disappeared the moment she noticed her friend was accompanied by two strange men, finally tuning in to the fact Emilia's expression on her tear-stained face was anything but contentment. "Oh no, something's happened! What's wrong?"

"Somebody…" Emilia's voice cracked and her shoulders shook, unable to get the words out.

Vogel took over. "Are you Miss Petra Berkner?"

"I am."

He held up his identification. "I'm Kriminalinspektor Vogel, and this is my partner, Kriminalassistent Stadler. May we come in?"

The woman's face paled and she stepped back, holding open the door. They entered the apartment and Vogel closed the door behind them. Petra led them into the living area and directed the now crying Emilia to the couch then sat beside her, putting an arm around the young woman's shoulders.

"What's happened?" she asked.

Vogel didn't volunteer the information. "Miss Schmitt informs us you have a spare key for her apartment."

"Yes, yes, I do." She pointed toward a key rack near the front door. "It's hanging right there."

Vogel frowned and walked over. Two of the keys were apartment keys. "Which one is for the apartment downstairs?"

"The one on the right."

Vogel removed his handkerchief then carefully lifted the key from the hook. He folded the cloth around it then put it in his pocket. "Were you aware that Miss Schmitt was away this past week?"

"Of course, not a day goes by that we don't speak. Isn't that right, Emilia?"

Emilia sniffed and nodded, saying nothing.

"And did you have occasion to go into her apartment while she was away?"

Petra visibly tensed. "No. Why? Was there a burglary?"

"No, nothing of the sort, but I need to know the truth. Were you in that apartment?"

Her shoulders slumped. "Yes."

Emilia gasped, pushing away from her friend. "Oh my God! How could you do that? How could you do such a thing?"

Petra stared at her, confused. "What do you mean? What did I do? All I did was go into your apartment for a few minutes."

Vogel held up a hand. "What did you do in the apartment?"

The woman's shoulders slumped. "Nothing nefarious, I assure you. I just was doing a favor for a friend."

"Just what were you doing?"

She smiled slightly and turned to the still horrified Emilia. "You know my friend Annie?"

Emilia stared at her. "Who?"

"Annie. She works with me at the factory. You met her once at Dieter Maier's party. Remember? That huge party we invited you to about six months ago?"

Emilia stared at her then her jaw dropped. She turned to Vogel. "I knew I recognized her! It's Annie. It's definitely her!"

Petra picked up on the change in tone in the room, and suddenly appeared nervous. "What's going on? Did something happen to Annie?"

"What's Annie's last name?"

"Dettman."

"And where do you work?"

"At the Adi Dassler Shoe Factory."

"And Miss Dettman worked there as well?"

"Yes."

"And how was she involved with Miss Schmitt's apartment?"

"Annie asked me if I could do her a favor. She's been seeing a boy and had fallen in love with him. Apparently, he lives with his parents and so does she, so they haven't had an opportunity to be together, if you know what I mean. She wanted to set up something romantic for their first time, and when I mentioned that Emilia was away, she asked if she could use the apartment. I didn't see the harm." She patted Emilia's knee. "I'm sorry. I just assumed it'd be all right with you once you heard their story. I was going to tell you when you got back."

Emilia sniffed and said nothing, though her demeanor suggested her friend was probably right.

Vogel sat. "Tell us exactly what happened."

"On Friday, Annie brought me a bag. It included wine, cheese, crackers, pâté, and a few other delicacies, along with some candles."

Stadler looked up from his pad. "A factory girl can afford stuff like that?"

Petra laughed. "Not at all. Annie's not really a factory girl. She works there with us, but she does it as her patriotic duty. Her father's a well-connected man."

It was Vogel's turn to look up. "Well-connected? As in well-connected within the Party?"

"Yes."

Vogel's mind raced for a moment then stopped when it reached a horrifying realization. "Annie's father wouldn't happen to be Hermann Dettman, would he?"

Her eyes shot wide. "Yes, as a matter of fact. That's exactly right."

Even the die-hard Nazi supporter Stadler shifted uncomfortably. Hermann Dettman was definitely a senior member of the Party, joining it shortly after its creation in the beerhalls of Munich. That meant he had plotted with the Führer himself, and it meant the pressure to solve this murder had just ratcheted up ten-fold. If they failed, it could be the end of everyone's career.

Or worse.

He ignored his uncertain future, returning to the task at hand. "So, she gave you this bag. What happened then?"

"Well, I came home, then I immediately went to Emilia's apartment, set everything up for their romantic evening, then left the key under the mat."

"And that's it?"

"Yes. I haven't heard from Annie yet to see how it went. I assume it went well because this morning, when I woke up, the key had been pushed under my door. I assume I'll hear on Monday if everything went the way she hoped it would."

"And how did she hope it'd go?"

"Like I said, she was hoping this would be their first time."

"First and last," muttered Stadler.

Petra's head spun toward his partner. "What does that mean?" Her face slackened. "Oh, my God, is she dead?"

Vogel nodded. "I'm afraid so, Miss. She was found murdered in Miss Schmitt's apartment this morning by the superintendent repairing the water heaters."

Petra's face paled and her eyes welled with tears. "Are you sure it was her?"

Stadler retrieved the photo and showed it to her. Petra cried out, both hands slapping against her chest.

"Can you confirm that this is Annie Dettman?"

"Y-yes, that's her."

"Now, you said you found the key under your door. Around what time was that?"

She shrugged. "I guess around eight this morning, give or take."

"And you heard nothing last night?"

She shook her head. "No. I had worked a long shift at the factory. After setting everything up for Annie, I came back upstairs, cooked my dinner, and then fell asleep. I don't think I woke up all night."

"Was she supposed to spend the night, or only the evening."

"The night."

"Wouldn't that have raised questions with her parents?"

Petra shook her head. "No, she told them she was spending the night with me."

"And they were fine with that?"

She shrugged. "It wouldn't have been the first time."

Vogel regarded her. "She arranged rendezvous like this before?"

Petra's eyes shot wide. "Oh, no! I mean, she actually stayed here. I'm the only one who doesn't live with their parents, so quite often we'll have sleepovers just so the girls can get a little time away."

"I see. What's the name of the boyfriend?"

She shrugged, holding up her hands. "I have no idea. Annie would never say. I got the impression that their relationship was a secret."

Vogel cursed to himself.

Of course. Why make it easy?

"Did she ever say anything about him? Was he tall, short, fat, thin, blond hair, black hair?"

"I'm sorry, she never said anything."

"Not even a first name?"

"Nothing. She made it quite clear to me that I wasn't to ask her any questions, because no one could know."

"Was he married?" asked Stadler.

Vogel regarded his partner.

An excellent question.

She shrugged. "Like I said, I know nothing, though I thought Annie would be a better person than to take up with a married man."

"She was about to have premarital sex," said Stadler.

She glared at him. "Lots of people have premarital sex, sir."

Vogel gave Stadler a look, silencing his partner. The last thing they wanted was a cooperative witness to be on the defensive. "We're not here to judge, Miss, we're here to find out who killed her, and right now, our prime suspect is whoever this young man was that she had a rendezvous with last night." He frowned. "And we actually don't even know he's a young man."

Petra shook her head again. "I'm sorry, I really wish I could help, but Annie was quite careful to tell no one anything. All we knew was that she was seeing somebody and was quite taken with him."

Vogel picked up on a crucial part of what she just said. "We?"

"Excuse me?"

"You said 'all we knew.' Who is 'we?'"

"Oh, a few of us at the factory that have lunch together and go out for drinks after work on Fridays."

He tore off a piece of paper from his pad and handed it to her along with his pen. "I'll get you to write down their names and addresses if you know them."

She quickly scribbled down three names and addresses, handing them back. He read them, none of the surnames standing out. "Are any of these people well-connected?"

Petra laughed. "They're just simple factory girls like me, who could only *dream* of being well-connected."

Vogel stuffed the list in his pocket then nodded toward Emilia. "Miss Schmitt is going to need some place to stay until her apartment can be cleaned up."

"Oh, you'll stay here, dear," said Petra, turning toward her friend. "You can stay here as long as you need to."

Emilia, who had apparently forgiven Petra for her transgression, smiled weakly. "Thank you."

Vogel put his pad in his pocket, turning to Emilia. "Your apartment is a crime scene for the moment, so there'll be people going through it. If there's anything you need, clothes, toiletries, just ask one of the officers and he'll coordinate it for you. If either of you remember anything that may be of importance, please call me at headquarters." He handed them each a card. "Day or night, you call."

"Yes, sir," they both echoed.

Vogel bowed his head slightly, then left the apartment, Stadler closing the door behind them as they walked toward the stairs.

"What do you think?" asked Stadler.

"I think if our victim is indeed the daughter of Hermann Dettman, then this case just got a lot more complicated."

Charlottenstraße, Berlin, Nazi Germany

Stadler waved his pad as he returned from the police callbox. "I've got Mr. Dettman's address." He handed the page to Vogel, who frowned the moment he read it.

"This isn't a residence, it's the Reich Chancellery."

"That's where he's insisting we meet him."

"Did you tell him what it's about?"

"Hell, no. I'm not telling a senior Nazi Party member that his promiscuous daughter has been murdered." He grinned at Vogel. "Rank has its privileges."

Vogel grunted. "Gee, thanks. Then I'll pull rank and delegate."

"You wouldn't dare."

Vogel enjoyed the horror on Stadler's face for a moment. "Fortunately for you, I wouldn't. But when you talked to him, didn't you tell him it was important that his wife be there as well?"

"I never got to speak to him."

Vogel stopped. "What?"

"I only reached his aide. I told the aide that it was critical we speak to Mr. and Mrs. Dettman as soon as possible concerning their daughter. He put me on hold then told me to come to the office. When I insisted, he simply repeated to come to the office then hung up."

Vogel rolled his eyes. "This is why I hate meeting with Party officials. They think the world revolves around them."

Stadler eyed him. "Doesn't it?"

Vogel chuckled. "Yes, I suppose you're right, it does. Did you request the files on her friends?"

Stadler shook his head. "Once I realized that Dettman was going to be a problem, I called headquarters. Sergeant Abel is going to take care of it."

"Good." Vogel climbed into their car when a uniformed officer rushed up, hailing him. Vogel rolled down the window. "What is it?"

"Glad I caught you, sir. We found something."

"What?"

"The missing items, we think."

Vogel's eyes narrowed at the doubt, but the excitement on the young man's face was evidence his fellow officers had found something they felt was important. He climbed out of the car and followed the officer into an alleyway less than a five-minute walk from the front door of Emilia Schmitt's building, finding several officers huddled around a recycling collection point, everything in the country collected for the war effort.

Sergeant Hellwig waved at him. "Sir, over here."

Vogel joined the throng. "So, Sergeant, what have you found for me?"

Hellwig pointed at a pile of cardboard. "You said the young woman's clothes and personal items were missing as well as a bottle of wine?"

A smile spread on Vogel's face. "Please, tell me you're not setting me up for a rather poor joke."

Hellwig chuckled as everyone stepped back. "No, sir. Have a look." He lifted a large piece of cardboard, revealing what they had found.

Vogel smiled at the sight. A woman's dress and undergarments were neatly folded, a purse lay on top, and an empty bottle of wine sat beside them, along with the remains of the same delicacies Petra Berkner had described. "And this is exactly how you found it?"

A young officer stepped forward, pointing at several cardboard boxes lying on the ground. "These were on top, sir. But as soon as I saw the clothing, I stopped."

"Excellent work. Too many people wouldn't have bothered to move anything, too concerned with getting their gloves dirty."

"Thank you, sir."

"Your name?"

"Rottmeister Farr."

Vogel made a note on his pad. "All right, Corporal, you can supervise while your friends collect everything in this alley and bring it to the lab."

Farr grinned. "Yes, sir!"

His comrades groaned and Vogel shrugged. "Hey, somebody has to do it." He turned to Hellwig. "Canvas the neighbors, see if they saw or heard anything, and make sure you get photographs of this area before you disturb it further. There's something peculiar about the way those things have been placed."

"You mean that the clothes are folded?"

"Exactly. Why would the killer carefully fold her clothes?"

Hellwig chewed his cheek for a moment. "If he knew her, and it was a crime of passion, then maybe he felt guilty and wanted to treat her belongings with respect."

"It's a possibility. Whatever the reason, there's certainly some meaning to it."

Stadler leaned closer to the carefully laid out items. "Maybe whoever did it is just a neat-freak. You know how some people are. They have to have everything exactly so."

"Another perfectly good explanation. Whatever the reason, it could mean something. Just get a few photographs then bring everything you can to the lab and we'll have them go through it. There might be something we're not seeing that can be tied back to the crime scene or the killer."

"Yes, sir."

Vogel turned on his heel and headed back to the car with Stadler.

"It *is* rather odd, isn't it?"

Vogel glanced at his partner. "What do you mean?"

"I mean the folded clothes."

"It is, but what I find odder is that they were dumped where they were."

Stadler eyed him across the roof of their car. "What do you mean? We've seen that before."

"Yes, we have, but all indications are that Annie was murdered by someone she thought cared for her. All evidence of her being in that apartment with someone was carefully cleaned up, and anything that person thought might help identify her or perhaps even lead back to him, was removed."

"What do *you* think it means?"

Vogel glanced at his partner as he started up the car. "What do *you* think it means?"

Stadler rolled his eyes. "More tests?"

"You're never going to become a good homicide detective if you don't learn to think for yourself."

Stadler sighed. "Well, if this wasn't a random act of violence, and the victim knew her killer, and even made love with that killer, and then the killer methodically slit her throat, watched her bleed out, then stabbed her multiple times…" He paused then frowned. "I don't know. There are elements here that would suggest premeditation, and there are elements that suggest a spur of the moment attack."

Vogel agreed. "Then take them one at a time. Let's assume premeditation. What contradicts that, and what supports that?"

"Well, just the very fact that the murderer knew the victim would suggest premeditation. The fact the throat was slit and he watched her bleed out, to me suggests premeditation as well. He intended to kill her, he knew how he was going to do it, because he likely brought the weapon with him, and he carefully cleaned up after himself, knowing he could be identified."

"Now, what contradicts the idea it was premeditated?"

"The multiple stab wounds would suggest some form of rage, I assume directed at her, though perhaps it was directed at himself for what he had just done. And if that were the case, then it would call into question whether it was premeditated."

"And?"

Stadler shrugged. "And?"

"And what about the clothing and the wine bottle we just found?"

Stadler's eyes shot up. "Why did he dump that stuff so close?"

"Exactly. If it were premeditated, I'm certain he would have taken everything with him and dumped them farther away, so there'd be no hope of us finding them before the garbage was picked up next week."

"But even if it wasn't premeditated, why dump things so close?"

"Perhaps the murderer lives in the area, and where he dumped the items is between the crime scene and where he lives."

Stadler's head bobbed. "That's an interesting idea. I suppose it narrows down the suspect pool a little bit."

"Perhaps, or perhaps the murderer panicked. He had the items, had planned on disposing of them far from the crime scene, but something spooked him, or he got too nervous and decided to dump the items early."

Stadler gave him a look. "So, what you're telling me is we actually know nothing."

Vogel laughed. "We don't know *nothing*. We know plenty. We just don't know what any of it means."

Stadler growled. "I fail to see the difference."

"The day you understand, is the day you're ready for this job."

Stadler stared at him as they drove. "You don't like me very much, do you?"

Vogel should have known better, but instead told the truth. "No. Is that a prerequisite?"

Stadler appeared genuinely hurt. "What did I ever do to offend you?"

"What do you think you did?"

Stadler tossed his head back. "Are you kidding me? Again with the questions?"

Vogel suppressed the delight he was taking in annoying his younger partner. "You didn't earn the job."

Stadler's eyes widened slightly. "What do you mean?"

"I mean, the only reason you're a detective in Homicide, working with me, is because of who your father is, not because of what you earned. You skipped the four-year program it takes to get to where you are."

Stadler frowned, his shoulders sagging, and Vogel sensed a little bit of truth might be about to reveal itself. "It wasn't my decision."

"What do you mean?"

"I'm not going to sit here and lie to you and say I wanted to go to the front. I didn't. The very notion terrifies me. But being a police officer, at least, seemed a respectable choice. It was my father who pulled strings to get me this more senior position. He didn't want me as some lowly police officer walking the beat. I know I don't deserve it, but you have to understand, I never asked for it."

"You could have said no."

"You *do* know who my father is, don't you?"

Vogel nodded, well aware Stadler Sr. was a general in the SS, and a dangerous man if crossed. The fact the Kripo were now part of the SS had facilitated his son's appointment without questions being asked.

"My father doesn't tolerate people saying 'no' to him, especially his family."

"Sounds like a difficult man to live with."

"Which is why the first opportunity I had, I moved out of the family home and got my own apartment."

Vogel felt a touch of sympathy for the young man for the first time since he had met him.

Stadler stared at him, his lip trembling for a moment. "You think I don't know what everyone says behind my back? You think I don't hear the snide remarks? See the dirty looks? You don't think at the end of each day, I don't go home crushed? I was supposed to have a great life because of who my father was. We have money and power. The family is respected. Yet my father didn't want me serving on the front, but still wanted me to serve. Like I said, I had no problem with that, but I wanted to start at the bottom and work my way up, like everyone else I'd be serving with. Instead, I was made a detective right out of police college, and a homicide detective to make it even worse. If I had the balls to challenge my father, I'd get myself busted back to recruit."

Vogel cranked the wheel, completing a left-hand turn. "If you're so concerned with what people think, why are you so gung-ho all the time?"

Stadler drew a knuckle under one eye. "You mean about the Reich and the Party and everything?"

"Yes."

"If everybody hated you, and didn't respect you, how would *you* protect yourself?"

Vogel pursed his lips. "You mean you want them afraid of you, so they don't take things too far?"

Stadler nodded, his voice barely a whisper. "Exactly."

Vogel thought of how he'd treated the young man since the moment he'd been assigned to him, and it hadn't been good. But now a little bit of context behind what had happened had him rethinking things. "So, it was all just an act?"

Stadler wagged a hand in front of him. "No, not completely. I am loyal to the Reich, to the Führer, and to the Party. Never get that wrong. I'm not like you, a Nazi in name only merely because your job required you to swear the oath."

Vogel tensed slightly. "You think I'm not loyal?"

Stadler regarded him. "Are you?"

Vogel chose his words carefully. "I'm loyal to my job, and I'm loyal to my country and the people I serve."

"Yet you say nothing about the Reich, the Führer, or the Party."

"If those three things have the best interests of the German people at heart, then by definition, I would be loyal to them as well."

Stadler shook his head, frowning slightly. "I thought we were having a moment where we told each other the truth."

"Some truths are better left unsaid."

Stadler grunted. "I can respect that. And don't worry, as long as you never betray any of the things I hold dear, you have nothing to worry about from me. I'm not a fool who thinks everyone is blindly loyal to the

Führer, nor am I foolish enough to think that everything he does is perfect. I may be young and not have lived through what you did, but I know enough to be fully aware that life in Germany was hell before the Führer saved us from the Treaty of Versailles and the Great Depression."

Vogel conceded that point. "Yes, things absolutely were worse. However, I fear should we lose this war, what once was, will pale in comparison to what is to follow."

Stadler stared out the window as they drove past a rubble-strewn street, an example of yet another allied bomber successfully reaching Berlin. "I have faith in the Führer. We shall be victorious in the end. All that stands between us and victory are the British, and they won't hold out much longer."

Vogel wasn't sure he agreed, though decided this conversation was entering dangerous territory. "Let's hope you're right."

Reich Chancellery

Wilhelmstraße, Berlin, Nazi Germany

Vogel sat with Stadler in the outer office of Hermann Dettman. They had been sitting for almost an hour, and if the man weren't who he was, Vogel would have kicked open the door and forced the meeting. He should be out investigating, not sitting here waiting for some arrogant fool to be notified that his daughter was dead, and to get answers to questions that might help lead to her killer. Every minute in a homicide investigation, especially in those first couple of days, were critical, a prime example the discovery at the recycling collection point, the contents of which were only a day or two away from being picked up and lost forever.

The intercom on the aide's desk buzzed, and *Obergefreiter* Friedel picked up the phone. "Yes, sir." He hung up, then rose. "Mr. Dettman will see you now."

"Finally," muttered Stadler.

Corporal Friedel turned on him. "What did you say?"

Vogel saved his young partner. "He said, 'finally.' We have a homicide to investigate, and we've just wasted an hour, an hour in which the murderer could have destroyed evidence or could have used to escape Berlin."

The young man's face paled slightly. "Murder? Who?"

"Your boss' daughter."

He was now white as a sheet. "Why didn't you tell me?"

Vogel wasn't about to explain procedure and instead decided a lesson should be taught. "When the police call, you don't mess around. If they say they need to meet with you urgently, then they mean it. We don't have time to waste on petty power trips."

Friedel bowed his head. "Yes, sir." He opened the door and led them inside. "Sir, this is Kriminalinspektor Vogel and Kriminalassistent Stadler."

Dettman tossed his pen on his desk then leaned back in his chair, sighing heavily as if this were the greatest inconvenience one could possibly suffer. "I'm a very busy man. What do you want?"

Vogel held his hand out and Stadler placed the photograph of Annie in it. Vogel stepped forward. "Is this your daughter?"

Dettman squinted at the photo, then retrieved his glasses from the desktop, pushing them onto his head. "Yes, of course it is." His jaw dropped. "Wait a minute, what's happened to her?"

Vogel handed the photo back to Stadler. "I regret to inform you that your daughter was found earlier today, murdered on Charlottenstraße." The man's face went ashen and his entire body slumped in his chair.

Vogel turned to Friedel. "Get him a glass of water and a shot of schnapps."

"At once!" Friedel left and returned a moment later, handing the glass and shot to Vogel.

"Take a few sips of water, sir," said Vogel. The glass was pressed into the man's hand, and after a moment, he took several sips, a little bit of color returning to his face. "Now the schnapps." The shot glass was placed in front of him and Dettman downed it then drew a deep breath. He put the empty shot glass down then took several more swigs of water before straightening himself.

"Thank you." Dettman returned to the image of the powerful man he was, though the white knuckles gripping the arms of his chair belied his true feelings. "Tell me everything."

"I have a couple of questions first that I need answered."

"Tell me what happened to my daughter!" snapped Dettman.

Vogel wasn't about to be led astray. "I will, sir, however, I need questions answered that aren't tainted by what I'm about to tell you."

The man growled. "Fine, ask your questions."

"Where was your daughter last night?"

"At a friend's. A can't remember the name. My wife would know."

"When were you expecting her back?"

He shrugged. "It's Saturday, so she isn't working. Normally she comes home by lunch after these sleepovers."

"Did your daughter have a boyfriend or a significant other in her life?"

"Absolutely not."

"You're certain?"

"Of course I'm certain. Are you suggesting my daughter leads some secret life I'm unaware of? She's a good Aryan girl who will marry someone that I approve of and no one else. Her generation will give birth to those who will rule the Reich when we are dead and gone."

"Heil Hitler!" shouted Friedel, snapping to attention and executing a perfect one arm salute. Stadler did the same out of habit, glancing sheepishly at Vogel, who remained standing at ease. Dettman half-heartedly tossed his right arm below the elbow in the air a few inches.

"Perhaps your wife is aware of somebody."

"My wife and I have no secrets when it comes to our daughter. If she were aware of Annie being involved with someone, she would have informed me immediately so that I could put an end to it. There are numerous young men who are very interested in marrying my daughter, not only because of her beauty, but because of who she is. She is my daughter, and she is pure Aryan stock, and I can assure you that any of the men worthy of her would never dream of going behind my back, for I would not only destroy them, but their fathers as well."

Vogel nodded. "I have no doubt, though I will still need to speak to your wife."

"Yes, of course. Now, tell me what happened to my daughter."

Vogel shifted uncomfortably. "You're not going to like this, sir, and I'm not sure if you want me to give you all the details."

"Tell me everything."

"Very well, sir. Your daughter's body was found in an apartment on Charlottenstraße by a superintendent repairing the water heaters. She was tied up naked in a bed, her throat slit, with multiple stab wounds to her torso."

Dettman shook in his seat as he struggled to maintain control. Friedel rushed out, returning a moment later with more water and another shot. They were both downed quickly, and Vogel tilted his head toward the door, Friedel taking the glasses again to refill them.

"Was she…was she raped? Was she violated?"

Vogel chose his words carefully. "She wasn't raped, sir."

Dettman picked up on his tone, lifting his head and staring at him. "But something did happen?"

"Yes, sir. According to a neighbor, your daughter arranged a rendezvous with someone she was in love with. All indications are that they had consensual sex, then she was murdered immediately afterward. This is why it's essential we find out who she might have been with."

Dettman said nothing as he continued to struggle. Despite his reputation, it was evident this man loved his daughter and was losing the control he was so accustomed to projecting. Vogel decided it was best to cut this meeting short, as he didn't want to humiliate the man and have it affect any future meetings.

"Sir, we're going to leave you now so that you can grieve the loss of your daughter. However, I would like to meet with you again, along with your wife and any household staff you may have later today. Is there a time that will be convenient for you?"

Dettman stared at nothing, then finally turned his head to check the clock on the wall. "I will meet you at my home in three hours."

"Very good, sir. Again, you have our condolences on the loss of your daughter." Vogel left the room with Stadler on his heels. Friedel handed them a piece of paper with the address for the residence, the young man clearly troubled.

"What do I do now?"

"You do your job. He's going to need help. I suggest you cancel all his appointments for the rest of the day."

"But some of them are with senior ministers."

"I'm sure they will understand."

"But it would project weakness. I can't just cancel these things. You know how it is."

Vogel frowned. He did know. Everything was image. Everything was based on how much strength and confidence you projected. Nobody wanted to align themselves with the weak. If one didn't show that one had the mettle to do what was needed, to do what was necessary, then one had no place among the upper echelon of the Party. He understood the trepidation of the young aide—it wasn't his place to put his superior's future in jeopardy.

"In five minutes, put your ear to the door. If you don't hear crying, then buzz him on your intercom and ask him if he would like you to cancel his meetings for the rest of the day and tomorrow. He'll most likely agree."

Friedel nodded. "Yes, sir."

Vogel handed him his card. "Should there be any problems, or you hear of anything that might assist us in finding out who the murderer was, let me know right away, day or night."

"Yes, sir."

Vogel left the office and headed for the stairs.

"I don't think I've ever seen a senior member emotional before," said Stadler, his voice hushed so as not to be overheard in the bustling hallways.

Vogel agreed. "Not unless they were angry or talking about Jews."

Stadler grunted. "Right, I forgot about that. So, do you believe him that he didn't know his daughter had a boyfriend?"

"Yes, I do, but my experience tells me that most fathers don't really know what's going on in their daughters' lives."

"Don't you have a daughter?"

Vogel chuckled. "Yes, I do. And puberty terrifies me every day. Thankfully, I have years before I need to worry about that. I want you to call into the office and have them pull all records on Annie Dettman. Birth, medical, employment, anything we have. Normally, I'd also pull the records on her parents, but one doesn't pry into the affairs of a senior Party official without the permission of someone more senior."

"Yes, sir," said Stadler as he jotted in his notepad. "What now?"

"Now, it's lunch." He glanced at the young man as they climbed into the car. "I'm heading home to have lunch with my family. Would you care to join us?"

Stadler's eyebrows shot up, the offer having never been made before. "I would be honored, sir."

"Good. Just remember who your audience is, and don't discuss the gory details of what we're working on."

"Yes, sir."

Vogel fired up the engine as Stadler glanced at him. "Can I ask you a question?"

"Of course."

"Why now?"

"Why now, what?"

"We've been partners for over a year. This is the first time you've invited me to your home for a meal. Most other partners dine together frequently."

"This is true, however today is the first time you've shown to me that you're worth dining with. You showed me a little bit of humanity."

Stadler turned his head and stared out the window. "I see."

Vogel heard the hurt in his young partner's voice, though didn't offer him any words of comfort. The way Stadler had been acting over the past year, he didn't deserve it, though Vogel was pleased that today was the first day since he had been assigned his new partner that he didn't entirely regret it.

There might be hope for you yet, young man.

Vogel Residence

Berlin, Nazi Germany

Sofia Vogel hummed happily as she efficiently assembled lunch for her family. These were stressful times and meager compared to the days preceding the war, but her husband had a good secure job, and they never went hungry. The rationing meant everyone was fed what the government felt they needed to remain healthy. There was a thriving black market friends of hers took advantage of, yet she couldn't, not with her husband being a police officer. Sometimes she felt a tinge of jealousy when she would join some of her friends for tea and they would show off by putting out a spread worthy of the late-thirties. She always bit her tongue and instead simply indulged more than she would typically, after sneaking a morsel or two into her purse to bring back to the children.

She had learned through a rebuke by her husband the first time she had offered him some of the ill-gotten gains, that he would have none of it, though he hadn't objected when it was given to the children. He would do anything for her or their children. He was a wonderful man who had never raised a hand to her. If it weren't for the war, their lives would be bliss as far as she was concerned. She came from a poor family and never needed much to be happy. All she needed was a solid roof over her head and three hearty meals a day with those she loved healthy. She still had most of that, though she had never counted on living in fear of constant bombardment, or running to air raid shelters, of hearing the weeping of mothers and wives as they received the impersonal telegram indicating another loved one had died at the front.

Why they were at war, she had no idea. The very notion sickened her. To her, how anyone could want to send their son to fight, illustrated, more than anything, the fundamental difference between men and women—though she could never express those opinions to anyone beyond her husband who shared her views in many ways.

His former partner had seen what was coming and fled the country before the war, now safely ensconced in the United States. She had wanted to follow him, however a bachelor fleeing was much less of an undertaking than a family with two young children.

She heard the key hit the lock and then the door to their apartment open. Her heart leaped and a smile spread as she dried her hands on her apron. She removed it then paused at another voice.

Did he bring someone?

"Sofia, I'm home. I brought Otto to join us for lunch."

She bristled. She had heard nothing good about Stadler, and had noticed without commenting that unlike her husband's former partner, Stadler was never invited into their home. What had changed had her curious. And she had to be the good wife. If her husband had decided his partner was now worthy to dine here, then she wouldn't question it, at least not now.

Tonight, however, there would be an inquisition.

She forced a smile then stepped out of the kitchen and joined her husband and his partner at the main entrance, suppressing the frown that threatened to emerge as she realized she now had to feed a fifth person somehow. Her husband stepped forward and gave her a peck on the cheek.

"Hon, you remember Otto?"

She extended a hand. "Of course."

Stadler smartly took the hand and bowed as any good Nazi would. "Ma'am, it's a pleasure. I hope it's not too much of an inconvenience that your husband invited me to your fine home." A hand emerged from behind his back with a brown bag. "I insisted that we stop so I could pick up a few items rather than take the food out of the mouths of your children."

Her opinion of the man instantly changed at his concern for her little ones. She took the bag and peered inside, her heart leaping. "This looks like an entire day's rations!"

He shrugged. "I'm not much of a cook, therefore I'm not much of an eater. I hate to let it go to waste, so do with it what you will. I'm sure whatever you create will be far more delectable than anything I could manage."

She smiled then extended a hand into their living area. "Please, make yourself comfortable. Lunch is almost ready." She exchanged a quick look with her husband, and it was clear he was in a good mood, and impressed with his partner's actions. The two men sat and she headed for the kitchen, emptying the bag onto the counter.

She cut off four thick slices from the loaf of bread Stadler had brought, re-assembling her husband's sandwich with the more generous pieces, then putting together a new one for their guest. Within minutes, she had a meal prepared that reminded her of the good old days. She brought the tray with the sandwiches into the dining area, then set an extra place. "Lunch is ready!"

The kids' feet pounded on the floor as they rushed from their bedroom. Her husband and Stadler entered the room, and she indicated where everyone should sit. She took her seat first, followed by their guest, her husband, and finally the children. The sandwiches were doled out, the beer and water were poured, grace was said by their guest, and she was pleased it wasn't a political speech followed by Amen, but instead a genuine heartfelt thanks to God.

Stadler took a bite of his sandwich and moaned as he chewed. He swallowed and wiped the corners of his mouth with a napkin. "Mrs. Vogel, I do believe this is the most delicious sandwich I have had in years."

She smiled. "Why, thank you, dear, the key is the seasoning. And please, call me Sofia."

"Thank you, ma'am."

She turned to her husband. "So, are things quiet at headquarters? I wasn't certain you'd be able to make it on time."

"Quiet, but not quiet enough. We're working a new case."

"Oh?"

"A young woman was found this morning."

"What happened to her, Daddy? Was she lost?"

Her husband smiled at their daughter. "Yes, she was."

"And you found her?"

"Yes, we did."

"That's good." Christina returned her attention to her sandwich, happily biting around the edges.

"Sounds like a difficult morning," said Sofia.

"We just came from meeting with the father. When we leave here, we'll stop by headquarters then head out to meet the entire household."

"I don't know how you can deal with that, day in and day out." She turned to Stadler. "How are you managing?"

He shrugged. "Sometimes it's difficult, especially the ones like today. But I guess you get used to it over time."

Her husband took a sip of his beer. "You grow accustomed to it, but you never get used to it. The day it stops affecting you, is the day you know you've worked the job too long, especially the ones like this morning."

She finished her sandwich, wiping her mouth. "Will you be home for dinner?"

Her husband shook his head. "No idea yet. Assume I won't be. If that changes, I'll try to give you a call."

"Don't worry, I'll keep yours warm in the oven."

He shot her a smile, the flash of his teeth always enough to send her heart aflutter.

She returned her attention to their guest. "So, Otto, this is the first time I've had a chance to interrogate you."

Stadler's eyes shot wide and he put a hand over his full mouth. "Ma'am?"

"You're a handsome young man. Do you have anyone special in your life?"

Stadler held up a finger, rapidly chewing then swallowing. "Not at the moment, ma'am. I did have someone, but her father was posted to Vienna and she went with him. And you know how long-distance relationships are. They're simply not worth it. All you're doing is postponing the inevitable."

She agreed. "This is true. Is your family from Berlin?"

"Yes, they are. I grew up not far from here as a matter of fact."

Her eyes narrowed slightly. "Really? I would have thought you'd have grown up in a much nicer neighborhood than this."

"This isn't exactly a slum, dear," commented her husband.

"That's not what I meant, and you know it. This is a quite fine neighborhood, however I assumed someone with your partner's family's stature would have grown up in a much finer neighborhood than this."

Stadler shifted in his seat uncomfortably. "We weren't always who we are today."

"Oh?"

Her husband cleared his throat and she glanced at him, the look he was giving her clear.

Drop it.

"Well, I think that's wonderful that your family was able to improve its station. The changes in the past ten years, I think, have improved many lives."

Stadler agreed. "Indeed. Many have been quite fortunate."

Her husband finished his sandwich then drained his beer. "I'm going to use the bathroom, then we should head out."

"Yes, sir."

Her husband left the room as his partner finished off his lunch. He rose. "Thank you, ma'am, for a delicious meal. I hope we can do it again soon."

She rose. "As do I."

Her husband returned. "Ready?"

Stadler nodded. "If I might use the facilities?"

"Of course, of course."

Her husband showed him the way and she began clearing the table as the children scurried back to their bedroom. She packaged up what remained of the rations that Stadler had brought, then joined them at the doorway. She held out the bag.

"Don't forget your food."

Stadler held out a hand, shaking his head. "No, that's my gift to you. Like I said, it'll just go to waste if it comes home with me. Enjoy it with my thanks."

She hugged the bag against her chest, realizing this would help provide for her family for the next several days. She might even put out a little extra with tea this afternoon for her friends. She'd have the girls envious. She suppressed a frown at the thought that if she did so, she would likely get accusations of being a hypocrite and taking part in the black market her husband opposed.

I just can't win.

She extended her hand to Stadler. "Thank you very much. You're most generous, and it was a pleasure to finally sit down and get to know you."

Another crisp handshake was delivered. "I assure you, ma'am, the pleasure was all mine."

Her husband gave her a kiss and the two men headed out the door. She locked it behind them then headed back to the kitchen with a smile, not only for the unexpected bounty she now carried, but for the fact her husband might finally become friends with his partner, something essential in his line of work.

If a detective couldn't trust his partner, then who could he trust?

Kriminalpolizei Headquarters

Prinz-Albrecht Straße, Berlin, Nazi Germany

Vogel strode into headquarters and the desk sergeant, *Wachtmeister* Abel, hailed him. "I have that information you wanted pulled together. It's sitting on your desk."

"Good work, Sergeant. Anything catch your eye?"

"Beyond the fact that a lot of pretty girls seem to work at shoe factories, nothing."

Vogel chuckled. "Perhaps you'd like to accompany us when we question them."

Abel grinned. "That sounds like a fantastic idea."

Vogel eyed him. "And would you like me to invite your wife?"

Abel tossed his head back, roaring in laughter. "You got me there, sir. Perhaps I'll just keep my ass parked right here."

Vogel continued toward his office. "That might be a wise marital move."

"Oh, there's a message for you, sir."

He turned. "What's that?"

"Medical Examiner Naumann wants to see you as soon as possible."

"Very well." He checked his watch then glanced at Stadler as they entered the office. "We should have time to squeeze him in." He sat at his desk and rifled through the files pulled together on Annie Dettman and her shoe factory friends. There wasn't much of interest. They were all young, late teens or early twenties, all had begun working at the shoe factory after the onset of the war, all lived in unremarkable neighborhoods, Petra Berkner the only one not living with family.

And none appeared to be connected directly to anyone of importance in the Party.

He would have to interview them individually. Hopefully, one of them would know who this mystery boyfriend was that Annie had been hiding. The question was whether they would volunteer the information. Luckily, he now knew that none of them were well-connected, which meant he could lean on them a lot harder than someone whose father was a Nazi Party official. It sickened him, but that was the world in which they now lived. It was a two-tiered justice system—one for the Nazis, the other for the proletariat. But that was their world, and as far as he could see, there was no changing it.

He set aside several files, then handed the rest to Stadler, who slipped them into his satchel. "Let's go see Naumann and find out what's so urgent. If we're lucky, maybe he's solved the case."

Stadler frowned. "That would be rather disappointing, wouldn't it?"

Vogel regarded him as he rose, heading out. "And why would that be?"

"Because then all our efforts would have been for nothing."

"You're forgetting one thing."

"What's that?"

"That our effort and our *glory*, which I think is what you're more concerned with, is unimportant. All that matters is that justice is served. I don't care if a shoeshine boy solves the murder and gets his face in the papers. All I care about is that the murderer is found and brought to justice, so that he can't do it again."

Stadler lowered his head slightly, his contrition evident. "You're right, sir. Sorry, sir."

Vogel slapped him on the back. "Don't worry about it. You'll figure this job out soon enough."

Stadler smiled, appreciative of the comforting words. "With your help."

Vogel approached Abel's desk, handing him the files on Annie's friends. "I think it's best I meet them at the factory. It'll save time. Arrange it for me, would you? Say in three hours?"

Abel nodded. "Consider it done."

"Can we expect you there?"

The old sergeant chuckled. "My wife would be serving my nuts on a platter if I went, sir."

Berlin-Mitte Morgue

Hannoversche Straße, Berlin, Nazi Germany

Vogel pushed open the swinging doors of the autopsy room and Naumann looked up from the body upon which he was working. "Another homicide?" asked Vogel.

"Good afternoon to you too."

Vogel chuckled "You're right, where are my manners? Good afternoon. A fine day we're having, isn't it?"

"Oh, very fine."

"Did you get bombed out of your home last night?"

"No, not at all, did you?"

"No, not at all. I feel lucky to be alive."

"You as well? I thought it was only me."

"It would appear that we're both lucky to be alive, as are all of the fine citizens of our great nation."

Stadler eyed them. "Are you two done?"

Naumann threw his head back and laughed. "Son, you need to learn to have a sense of humor in this business, or looking at death day in and day out is going to eat you alive." He jabbed a scalpel toward the body in front of him. "This poor fellow died from a massive heart attack when his wife walked in on him piledriving the housekeeper. I've been asked to find out if there's any way to blame the housekeeper and not the wife."

Stadler eyed him. "Why would the wife get in trouble? Wouldn't it be his fault?"

Naumann chuckled. "Oh, this isn't about the truth, it's all about saving face."

"What could they possibly think you'd find?"

"You're asking for logic from our leaders?"

Vogel gave Naumann a look, and he forced a smile as he no doubt remembered who his audience was. He jabbed his scalpel at the young partner. "Ah, got you there, didn't I? Like I said, you need to learn to have a sense of humor, in this case, gallows humor. But in all seriousness, what I said happened did actually happen. What they want is a possible other explanation for why he died other than a heart attack from having the shit scared out of him by a wife who was home early from tea. Nobody likes their people dying from being caught with their pants down. It's embarrassing not only to their memory, but to the Party."

Stadler grunted. "Yes, I suppose. Have you found anything?"

"No, though the official record will show he died from a massive stroke unrelated to any physical activity and more likely related to overwork."

Vogel shook his head, smiling. "So, he worked himself to death instead of screwed himself to death?"

"See, he gets it."

Stadler stared at the body. "Does this happen often?"

"What? Party officials dying during sex with their house staff?"

"No, I mean falsifying death records."

"It depends on who's on the table and where they are in the Party hierarchy."

"But isn't that unethical?"

Naumann stared at Stadler, flabbergasted. "You expect ethics from—"

Vogel saved him. "We're on a schedule here. What is so important that you had my desk sergeant telling me to get down here right away?"

Naumann stared at Stadler a moment longer then switched his attention to the matter at hand. "Yes, I was going over our victim, literally with a fine-tooth comb, and found something potentially of interest."

"What's that?"

"Well, our victim has blond hair, and I found the hair of a brunette on her body."

"Could it just belong to the woman who actually lives there?"

Naumann shrugged. "I don't know. What color hair does she have?"

"Black, I think." Vogel turned to his partner. "Do you remember?"

"Definitely black, sir."

"Well, this hair was brown," said Naumann.

"Are you saying that someone else was in the room?"

"I'm not saying anything. All I'm saying is that there was a brunette's hair on the victim's body, but there's no way to tell whether it was put there during the murder or a month ago. It's where I found it that could be of significance."

"Where did you find it?" asked Stadler.

Naumann tilted his head toward the young man and then directed his eyes at Stadler's crotch. The young man stared down, puzzled, then suddenly looked up. "Oh, I see."

"Like I said, fine-tooth comb. Now again, it could be accidental contamination, so in an attempt to rule that out, I sent one of my interns back to the crime scene to go over it—"

"With a fine-tooth comb?" asked Vogel.

"You're two for two, Kriminalinspektor. Yes, he went over everything in the bedroom and the apartment, and the only hairs he found were a few that matched our victim, and a normal amount that were black."

Vogel turned to Stadler. "Make a note to ask Miss Schmitt how often she cleans her apartment, and get a list of her brunette friends that might have been in the apartment in the past two months."

Stadler scribbled down the notes. "Yes, sir."

Vogel turned back to Naumann. "So, what you're suggesting is because only the one brown hair was found, and because of where it was found, that there's a third person involved?"

"Like I said, I'm not suggesting anything, I'm just telling you the facts, conjecture is your job."

Vogel eyed him. "Funny, I thought the truth was."

"What's the truth these days?"

Vogel decided Naumann's mouth would get him in trouble with his devout Nazi partner if he let him flap his gums too much longer. "Anything else the hair tells us?"

"Just that it belonged to a Caucasian, was brown, and long. Over six inches."

"So, it belonged to a woman, not a man," concluded Stadler.

Naumann wagged a finger. "Wolfgang, what are you teaching this boy? You should know that you can't tell someone's sex by their hair."

"But you said it was long."

"I've seen some ruffians in my day with long hair. Never jump to conclusions. It might just bite you on the ass."

"Do you have anything else for us?" asked Vogel.

"No, just that."

"All right, we're off to interview the victim's family and household staff."

"Have fun."

"I always do." Vogel threw open the swinging doors and headed down the corridor to the parking lot, Stadler beside him.

"Do you think he's right?"

Vogel glanced at his partner. "Right about what?"

"That there was a third person there?"

"I never heard him say that. I heard him say that he found a brown hair on our victim's groin, and it was the only brown hair that happened to be found in the apartment."

"All right, fine. What do you think it means?"

"I think it means there was a third person in the apartment."

Stadler groaned. "Is everybody your age deliberately difficult?"

Vogel shrugged. "Only with people younger than us. It makes us feel superior."

"All it does is make you all assholes, if you ask me."

Vogel chuckled. "Then it's working." He climbed into the car, starting the engine. "The hair could be completely innocent. It's where it was found that suggests there's something more here."

Stadler chewed his cheek for a moment. "Let's assume there was another woman there. What does that mean?"

Vogel put the car in gear and pulled away. "It could mean one of several things. Either there's another victim out there, there's a survivor out there, or there's another guilty party out there."

"Man or woman."

"Anything is possible. There's no evidence that a second person was killed there. It wouldn't make sense for the murderer to kill Annie and then take the second person with him while he hastily disposed of her personal items. I can't see any conceivable way that such a scenario could have occurred."

"They escaped?"

"That's possible, though if you were escaping a brutal murderer in an apartment building, wouldn't you be raising holy terror to try and draw attention to what was going on?"

Stadler frowned. "According to our canvassing, none of the neighbors reported hearing anything."

"Exactly."

"Perhaps they escaped without the murderer knowing, and were trying to be stealthy about it."

"Yes, that's a possibility as well, but wouldn't you have gone to the police?"

Stadler shook his head. "I'm too afraid to go to the police."

"Why are you too afraid?"

His partner stared out the window and Vogel let him think, his own ideas formulating. Stadler's head swung toward him.

"Because I don't think the police can help me."

"Why can't they help you?"

"I don't think the police can help me because of who the murderer is!"

Vogel smiled slightly. "Interesting theory. Run with it."

Encouraged, Stadler did just that. "The murderer is somebody important or well connected. You know that if you go to the police and they investigate, if they discover who the murderer is, they'll pin it on you to protect the murderer. Just like Naumann was under orders to change the cause of death, you can't run that risk, so you just go home and say nothing, and hope the murderer doesn't come for you."

"Excellent theory, and I agree it's a definite possibility, however, let's see if we can poke some holes in that.

Stadler shrugged. "It seems pretty solid to me."

"Well, take it further."

"Huh?"

"Take it further. You're the third person, you're sitting at home, keeping your mouth shut, and that's all well and good. But what's the murderer doing?"

"Sitting at home and hoping he got away with it?"

"You saw that fatal wound to the neck. That was cold and calculated. If you're willing to kill somebody like that, are you going to stop at one?"

"There are the stab wounds, though, that suggest there was rage."

"Yes, and I don't really have an explanation for that."

Stadler's eyes shot wide. "What if it was the third person who did those?"

Vogel's head bobbed at the idea. "Excellent thinking. So, two murderers rather than two victims."

"It's possible, isn't it?"

"It's definitely possible. Though does it fit the facts we know? She was there for a romantic evening. She made love with someone we assume was the young man she was there to meet."

Stadler held up a finger with a wry smile. "A man. We don't know if he was young."

Vogel conceded the fact. "You're right, I misspoke." He continued. "When does the second murderer arrive? He or she doesn't just show up unexpectedly, because it's not the victim's or the murderer's apartment. The second murderer would have had to have been invited by one of them. If it was a woman that arrived, then either it was Annie who invited her, or her boyfriend, shall we say, invited her, perhaps for a sexual encounter a little more out of the ordinary."

Stadler's eyes shot wide. "I've heard of that." He frowned. "The very idea has no appeal. I have enough trouble satisfying one woman, let alone two."

Vogel chuckled. "You and me both."

"But would Annie have been into that?"

"We don't know. I've seen plenty of occasions where a young woman has done anything the man she loves has asked because she fears losing him. However, if a sexual encounter had happened in that bed with three people, whether that third was a long-haired man or a woman, I would think there would have been more than one hair left behind. I don't think the third person was there for a sexual encounter."

Stadler agreed. "I think you're right. So then why were they there?" His eyes shot wide again. "Wait a minute! We're assuming that the young man, sorry, the man that Annie was there to meet was the murderer. What if he's the second victim, and didn't go to the police for the same reason? What if he escaped, and because he knew who the third person was and how well connected they were, he didn't want to say anything? Or maybe he's well connected himself?"

"Or there's another possibility," said Vogel. "Annie herself is well connected. Either scenario could mean the second or third person is a murderer or victim. Either way, nobody would want to be associated with what happened because of who her father is, no matter how innocent they were. They would know that he could destroy them."

Stadler stared at him. "So what are we saying? We've got a third person, possibly, who might be a woman or a man with long hair, who might have been invited by Annie or her friend, who probably didn't have a sexual encounter with them, who might be a second victim or the murderer, any of whom could be well connected, explaining why no one else has come forward?"

Vogel nodded firmly. "Exactly."

"Well, how the hell does that help us?" cried Stadler.

Vogel laughed. "Welcome to police work, my friend. First, you come up with all the possibilities, and then you start eliminating them one by one. And what did the great Sherlock Holmes say?"

Stadler rolled his eyes. "I don't know. Watson, where's my cocaine?"

Vogel snorted. "No, he said something to the tune of, 'when you have eliminated the impossible, whatever remains, however improbable, must be the truth.'"

"Oh yeah. Forgot that one. So, if you're Sherlock Holmes, does that mean I'm Watson?"

Vogel looked at him askance. "No, I think that makes you Mrs. Hudson."

Outside the Dettman Residence

Berlin, Nazi Germany

Annie had told him where she lived, though he had never dared to come onto the property. He had, on several occasions, stood across the street when she'd be coming back from work, and they would share a moment of her staring out her bedroom window at him, he at her. Only young lovers could be satisfied with such stolen moments, and as he now stood across the street, staring at her empty window, his shoulders shook with the realization there would never be any more moments to steal.

Annie was gone forever, and he was responsible.

Something inside him had compelled him to come here, and he wasn't sure why. Deep in the back of his mind, he had the notion of seeing her parents and telling them what had happened, and to apologize for what he had done. They would then at least hear the truth from him, someone who had loved their daughter, rather than some strange police officer they had never met, giving them the cold, hard facts. They should know that Annie was with someone she loved in her final moments, and they should know that that person had committed the ultimate sin.

She was dead because of him.

He stared at the bloody knife still gripped in his hand. He couldn't bring himself to throw it away, the blood on the blade the last connection he had to what was supposed to have been his future. Yet, he couldn't carry it around with him. He stared at the razor-sharp edge, then at his wrists, and debated slicing them, ending his suffering.

Yet if he did so, justice couldn't prevail.

He watched as a car pulled into the yard, two men in long trench coats climbing out, their demeanor suggesting they were the very police he had hoped wouldn't be the ones revealing what had happened. It was too late, and now he had no clue what he should do. He could walk over there right now and turn himself in and hope they would give the truth a chance. He could end it all right now by slitting his wrists. Or he could give in to his instincts and run.

He stared once again at the knife and dropped it at his feet before committing to the primal urges of self-preservation.

Dettman Residence

Berlin, Nazi Germany

Vogel pulled to a stop in front of the impressive house, a house he had no doubt was given to Hermann Dettman by the Party, its original owners left uncompensated. So many houses across Germany that had once belonged to successful Jewish families had been looted and emptied, handed over to "deserving" Nazis. The entire notion disgusted him. He couldn't say he had any Jewish friends before the Nazis started coming for them, but he could also say he had never had a problem with any of them. They typically didn't mix that much socially, and certainly wouldn't have associated with a police family, not since Nazism had taken hold.

The speculation between him and his partner about Annie's murder had continued most of the way here, and no matter how much they tried to debunk each theory, the only one they had successfully eliminated was that a threesome had occurred.

Vogel knocked on the door, and a member of the household staff promptly opened it. They were shown to the drawing room where they waited several minutes before Annie's parents appeared. They both rose and Dettman introduced his wife, Johanna, then everyone returned to their seats except for Stadler, who milled about the room as he typically did. It was an effective way of making people uncomfortable, and it could sometimes cause them to slip up when their attentions were split between protecting themselves and wondering just what the hell the young man was doing.

Vogel began the interview. "Mrs. Dettman, I assume your husband has informed you of what has happened?"

It was a redundant question, the woman's eyes red, her nose sniffling, a handkerchief clenched in her hand as she continually dabbed at the corners of her eyes. "Yes."

"As I informed your husband, we have a witness who says your daughter was meeting a man last night for a, shall we say, romantic interlude."

Johanna firmly shook her head. "Nonsense. She was at Petra Berkner's last night."

"Did she tell you that?"

"Yes. When she came home after work, she told me of her plans."

"I'm afraid that was a ruse."

Johanna glared at him. "That can't be! Our daughter is a good girl!"

"That may be, however, sometimes good girls do stupid things for boys they love. Our witness assures us that your daughter was very much in love with whoever she was meeting. And, I realize this may be indelicate, however she had planned to have sexual relations with him last night, and medical evidence confirmed she did just that."

Dettman exploded from his chair. "She was raped! If she had sex last night, it was certainly not consensual!"

Vogel remained calm. "Sir, I know we all want to think the best of our children. I have two of my own, however I assure you, if she were raped, the evidence would have shown that. You can take comfort that it was your daughter's first time, that it was consensual, and that she didn't suffer that particular humiliation."

Dettman dropped back onto the couch, his shoulders rolled inward in defeat. "I guess I didn't know my daughter at all."

"I think at that age, sir, few of us do. However, with this new awareness, I'll ask you again, sir, and I'll ask you, ma'am, is there anyone you can think of that your daughter had her eye on, anyone that she may have mentioned seeing just casually out with friends, going to a movie, a walk in the park? Someone she might have met at a club that she was a member of, some organization, church, anyone you can think of, or anyone who expressed an interest in her, especially if the idea particularly revolted her. Quite often, a young person will overreact when asked, to try and cover up their true feelings."

Both of them shook their head, Johanna speaking first. "For the life of me, I can't think of anyone, though I do know there were a lot of young men who were definitely interested. She's a very beautiful girl." She stifled a cry. "*Was* a very beautiful girl."

"Perhaps I could get you to put together a list of these young men who've expressed an interest in your daughter, and any other names you can think of, as well as any clubs or organizations she belonged to, what church she attended, any place you think she could have been over the past several months where she might have met her murderer."

Dettman nodded. "Yes, we'll put that together for you. Is tomorrow morning good?"

"Absolutely. Now, I'd like to talk to your household staff."

"What for?"

"Quite often, they notice things or hear things that parents don't."

"You mean they eavesdrop? I assure you, we have only loyal Germans here."

"No, that's not what I mean. What I mean is that staff are ignored, so quite often they're in a room and conversations continue as if they aren't there. They're not eavesdropping, however they can't simply stop their ears from functioning,"

Dettman grunted. "This is true, even I'm guilty of it. Perhaps I should rethink things."

Vogel said nothing.

Dettman picked up a bell sitting on the end table and rang it. The door opened a moment later, a young woman in a maid's outfit stepping inside. "Assemble the staff in the front hall immediately."

"Yes, sir." She closed the door and Dettman rose, Vogel following suit. He handed the man his card. "Should you think of anything, contact me, day or night. And the headquarters address is there. If you could have one of your staff bring over those details in the morning, it will greatly assist our investigation into your daughter's murder."

"I'll see to it." Dettman eyed the card. "Vogel. The last name isn't familiar to me. Are you a member of the Party?"

He was being assessed. Was he a loyal German, a loyal Nazi, someone who could be trusted that should the Party be embarrassed, he could be counted on to protect those more important than him? "Of course, sir." He caught a sideways glance from Stadler, who wisely kept his mouth shut.

Dettman turned his attention to Stadler. "And your name is?"

"Otto Stadler."

Dettman's eyes narrowed slightly. "And your father?"

"Klaus."

Dettman pursed his lips, his head bobbing in appreciation. "I know him. A good man. A good Nazi."

"Thank you, sir."

"Say hello to him for me."

"I shall, sir. And I'm sure I can speak for him when I say you have his and my entire family's condolences for your loss."

Dettman bowed his head. "Thank you, young man, well said." He wagged a finger at Stadler as he turned to Vogel. "I think you've got a good partner there."

Vogel gave Stadler a bemused smile. "He's shaping up into one, yes, sir."

There was a knock at the door and the young woman poked her head inside. "Sir, the staff is assembled."

"Excellent."

Dettman held out a hand toward the door. "Shall we?"

Vogel didn't move. "It would be preferable if we spoke to them alone, sir. They're more likely to speak freely if you and your wife aren't in the room."

Dettman frowned, but agreed. "Very well. We have nothing to hide, though apparently our daughter did. Let's hope that one of them can help bring her killer to justice." He sat back down beside his wife who collapsed into his arms. Vogel followed the maid out of the room with Stadler.

"What's your name and position?"

"I'm the chambermaid. Heidi Gerich," she replied as she led them to the main entrance where three other staff members stood.

"Is this it?"

"Yes, there's only the four of us."

Vogel found that hard to believe. "No one is off sick? No one comes in for the late shift?"

Her jaw dropped. "Oh, I'm sorry, sir. I misunderstood. No, this is everyone on the day shift. There are two for the night shift. I can get you their names and contact information."

"Do that. Anyone off sick?"

"No."

"Anyone let go in the past two months?"

"No."

A man behind her cleared his throat. "There was Karl."

Her eyes shot wide. "Oh my, I forgot about Karl. Yes, he was let go about two weeks ago."

"What for?"

"I'm sure I don't know."

Vogel eyed her. "Whenever someone says that, it means they do know. I assume you're all aware of what happened to young Annie last night?"

Everyone became more subdued than they already were, his years of experience suggesting something else was going on besides the shock of a murder. "Yes, sir," said the young woman. "We're all aware, and we're all devastated by the news. She was such a good girl, always very friendly, always very respectful. We'll miss her deeply."

"If that's true, then I would assume you would all want her murderer brought to justice."

Everyone nodded, though none made eye contact.

"Of course, sir," said Heidi finally. "We've already discussed it among ourselves, and none of us could think of anything that might be helpful. Miss Dettman was a simple girl. This lifestyle wasn't one she was born into." She lowered her voice considerably. "Nor was it what her parents were born into, if you know what I mean."

"Tell me about this Karl. Why was he let go?"

"Like I said, sir, I'm sure I don't—"

"And like I said, when I hear those words spoken, it tells me somebody knows something, otherwise nobody would be uncomfortable. All I see is shifting feet and eyes looking anywhere but my direction. What did Karl do that was so egregious it got him fired?"

"Just tell him," grumbled a man whose attire suggested he was a groundskeeper. "He's going to find out eventually."

Heidi sighed. "Very well. He was caught doing something inappropriate."

The groundskeeper growled again. "That's not telling him."

Vogel turned to the man. "And you are?"

"Ernst Handt. I'm the groundskeeper." He stepped forward. "That young fool has doubled my workload because of what he did. The Dettmans are terrified to hire a replacement. They don't want any more young men near their daughter after what happened. Frankly, I don't blame them. She was too beautiful and too innocent to be allowed near any man unaccompanied."

Vogel's eyes narrowed slightly. "You had a young man working here during a time of war?"

"He wasn't able to fight. Some childhood injury to his leg caused him to walk with a limp. He was my assistant for the past two years. He was a little slower to get from Point A to Point B, but he was a capable, diligent worker."

"And what was it that he did that merited termination?"

"I had him pruning one of the trees, so he was up on a ladder in front of Miss Dettman's bedroom window. Apparently, she was changing and spotted him ogling her. She screamed and there was quite the ado after that."

"Did he admit to what he had done?"

"No, he denied it. He claimed he was merely doing his job when he heard her scream, that he wasn't even aware he was in front of her window."

Stadler cleared his throat. "That seems rather unlikely, if he's been here for two years."

Heidi shook her head. "He'd only ever been in the house through the staff entrance, and would never have been in any of the main living areas, and certainly not the bedrooms upstairs. There's no way he could have known."

"And you said this happened about two weeks ago?" asked Vogel.

"Yes. Saturday before last, I believe. Mr. Dettman fired him immediately."

"And what was Karl's reaction?"

"He was quite distraught."

"Was he angry?"

"If he was, he certainly didn't show it."

"Describe Karl's hair."

Eyebrows rose everywhere.

Handt stared at him. "What kind of question is that?"

"A rather simple one. His hair. Was it short, long, brown, blond?"

"Oh. Short, blond."

Heidi shook her head. "No, it was short and sandy. A blond-brown mix."

Handt shrugged. "What do I know of hair? Grass, now *that* I can tell you everything about. Hair, I couldn't care less. My wife cuts it once every two weeks only to keep me presentable. Otherwise, I'd keep it long, like some of those ruffians I've seen about."

Vogel regarded him. "Ruffians?"

Handt shrugged again. "You know, ne'er-do-wells who somehow found a way to escape service to their country."

"And were any of them around here?"

"I might have seen one or two around, but I've never paid them any mind."

"But you've seen Annie with a long-haired man?"

"No, not with her, just in the area. And I wouldn't exactly call any of them men."

"What do you mean?"

"You know what I mean."

Vogel did, and if it were true, it might explain the lack of evidence that there had been a sexual encounter with a third person if his predilections didn't tend toward women. He looked at the others. "Have any of you seen any long-haired men with Miss Dettman?"

Heads shook, though it was clear to him these people knew more than they were willing to volunteer as a group. "I think it's time for individual interviews." He turned to Stadler. "Why don't you interview Mr. Handt first, and I'll take Miss Gerich? The rest of you remain here until you're called for."

Heidi pointed to a hallway. "The servants' wing is this way. There are rooms there that we can use."

They followed her, splitting off into separate rooms. Vogel closed the door and found himself in what must be the staff dining area. He motioned for Heidi to sit, and she did. He sat across from her and pulled out his notepad.

"So, tell me what has all of you on edge."

The young woman's shoulders slumped. "How did you know?"

"I've been a homicide detective for years, and I know when someone's holding back. It's time to tell me everything. You don't want me thinking you're involved."

She gasped, a hand darting to her mouth. "How could you say such a thing? Annie was always good to me, and I always treated her with the utmost respect. Like I said, she wasn't born into this life and didn't want any part of it. She always felt guilty when I was cleaning her room or making her bed, always insisting on helping me."

"And her parents, how did they treat you?"

"Well enough, I guess. The missus is the worst. Her husband just ignores me and always leaves the room if I'm there, but I think his wife feels she deserves what she has, and that people like me are beneath her despite the fact I overheard a conversation that she used to be a housekeeper in Munich before the Nazis came to power and dragged her husband higher in society." She gasped at her bluntness. "Please, don't tell anyone I said these things!"

Vogel smiled. "You have my word." He continued. "But the staff was generally treated well?"

"As good as any other household, I would say."

"Then they've done nothing to merit their daughter being murdered?"

Her eyes shot wide. "Of course not! I can't imagine anything that anyone could do that would merit such a thing!"

"And did anyone besides Karl pay any special attention to Miss Dettman?"

She shook her head vigorously. "No, and I don't believe Karl did either. Even Annie didn't want him fired, but her father refused to listen. He's very overbearing when it comes to such things."

It was an interesting choice of words. "In what way? What do you mean by 'such things?'"

"I mean with respect to his daughter's future."

"You mean in marriage?"

"Exactly."

"Explain."

She leaned forward, lowering her voice. "Well, like I said, if it weren't for the Nazi Party, this family would never be living the life they are. And things can be, shall we say, fleeting in today's world."

Vogel nodded but said nothing, preferring to allow the woman to speak freely.

"We've all heard things here and there, and it's my opinion and that of the others, that he's desperate to have her marry not only someone well connected within the Party, meaning someone with power, but to marry someone rich."

Vogel leaned back, folding his arms. "So that if something goes wrong with Mr. Dettman's career, they'll have their daughter to maintain their lifestyle?"

She shrugged. "It's what everyone here thinks."

It did make sense. If Johanna Dettman had been a housekeeper, then it meant Dettman had been in a profession that didn't pay him enough to support the family. His experience told him that those who tasted wealth, when starved of it, would stop at nothing to feed again at the trough of the rich. He could understand why Dettman would want to protect himself from a future of poverty, though to essentially prostitute one's daughter as a safety net for one's comfort was disgusting.

But her answer posed several new questions. "Was Annie aware of her father's plans for her?"

"Yes."

"And what did she think of them?"

"She wouldn't dare challenge her father, though I do remember overhearing a bit of an argument at dinner about a year ago. Apparently, she wanted to go out with friends, and when he heard that several boys would be with them, he refused permission. I didn't hear everything, but I did hear her say something about not wanting to marry some old man."

Vogel frowned. "Do you think he would make her marry someone much older?"

"I think that man would do anything." She lowered her voice further. "He is a Nazi, you know."

Vogel smiled slightly. "Oh, I know."

His words put her more at ease, the arms folded across her chest lowering. She sighed. "I don't know who killed her, sir. I can't think of anyone who would want to hurt her. Karl was just an innocent boy. Even if he did look, could you blame him? She was beautiful, and young men that age, if they see a naked woman, they're going to look. It's instinct. They can't help it, but it doesn't mean they'd ever act on it, especially Karl. My God, if he tried to chase her down, she could escape him at a brisk pace."

The woman had a point. "Let's forget Karl and return for a moment to her father's future plans for her. Do you know how Mrs. Dettman felt about them?"

"Oh, she was definitely in support from what I overheard. I wouldn't be surprised if it were all her idea, to be perfectly frank. That woman is obsessed with this lifestyle. I don't think there's anything she wouldn't do to keep herself in it. She loves to entertain, and I hear her boasting all the time about her husband's position and connections, who they had dinner with, who they ran into at some function. To her, it was all about the names."

"How do you think she would react if she found out Annie had a boyfriend that she didn't approve of?"

Heidi inhaled rapidly, her hand darting to her chest. "Oh, I'd hate to think! It would definitely be treated as some sort of betrayal. I was cleaning the room one day, and the two of them were sitting on the bed while she brushed Annie's hair, talking about how important it was for her to maintain her virtue in order to be worthy of her future husband."

Vogel scratched his chin as his mind raced. "What color hair would you say Mrs. Dettman has?"

"Brown."

His head slowly bobbed. "Yes, that's what I would call it as well."

She eyed him. "Why do you keep asking about hair?"

He shook his head. "None of your concern. Now, back to these young ruffians as your groundskeeper described them. Do you know any of whom he's talking about?"

"I can't say I've seen any on the grounds. The only friends I knew Annie to have were at the factory where she worked. She's had several young women over for tea, but I've never seen a young man. Her parents would never have allowed it. Actually, I'm surprised they let her work at the factory. They weren't in support of it at first, but when Mr. Dettman found out several other prominent Nazi families had their children working at factories to support the war effort, he felt in order to save face, he had to do the same, so he allowed it."

"And among the friends of the Dettmans, are there any young men with long hair? Their sons? Nephews?"

"Absolutely not. These are all proper Nazis. Everyone has short hair."

"Any with an eye for Annie?"

"Oh, they all had eyes for Annie. The only reason they were ever brought here with their parents was to make introductions. It was almost as if there'd be a bidding war."

"And what was Annie's reaction to this?"

"She was polite about it, though I don't think she cared for it much."

"Would it surprise you to know that she had someone she loved very deeply in her life?"

Her eyes widened and then a smile slowly emerged. "It would surprise me, but it would also delight me." She clasped her hands in her lap, wringing them repeatedly. "Can you tell me how she died?"

"I'm afraid I can't reveal any details about the case. Can you think of anything else relevant?"

She shook her head. "Not at the moment, no."

"I think you can."

Her cheeks paled. "I'm sure I can't."

He smiled. "You're all on edge. What is it that you're not telling me?"

She sighed. "You're right, sir, I forgot." She glanced about, as if to make sure they were still alone, then lowered her voice. "We just discovered a very expensive bottle of wine is missing, along with some delicacies."

"Such as?"

"Pâté, cheese, crackers, a few other things. It's the wine that's the concern."

"And why does this have the staff on edge."

"We haven't told Mr. Dettman yet. Once he and the missus find out, there will be hell to pay. They're liable to fire all of us if the perpetrator doesn't come forward."

Vogel smiled at her. "Tell the staff to rest easy. It was Annie who took those items for her rendezvous last night."

Heidi's eyes shot wide. "Oh, thank God!" She calmed herself. "Will you, umm, tell Mr. Dettman for us?"

"Should it become necessary. However, I suggest you tell him yourself, and that you also tell him that the missing items match what was found near the crime scene." He handed her his card. "If you think of anything, let me know, day or night."

"Yes, sir."

"All right, you can leave now and send the next one in. Don't forget to get me the details on Karl and the night shift. And if you can, get me a photo of Annie. I hate having to show her autopsy photo when we're questioning witnesses."

"Yes, sir."

She left and he leaned back, folding his arms and closing his eyes as he thought of what had just been said, and how her answers had given him a horrifying theory as to who the third person might be.

Wilhelmine Ring Residential District

Berlin, Nazi Germany

He primed the pump several times before water finally gushed from the well. He washed the dried blood from his hands, the sight of it flowing once again sickening, the horrors he had witnessed last night relived once again. He was starving, on the run now for over half a day, with no ultimate destination.

And he had no idea if anyone was even searching for him.

He and Annie had kept their relationship a secret from everyone. She had friends he assumed she confided in, and he was well aware they were in someone else's apartment. Annie had confided after he arrived that it had already been prepared by someone else that lived in the apartment directly above her. He was racking his brain, trying to remember the name of her friend, as Annie might have also trusted her with his name, yet it didn't matter.

What was he going to do? Kill her?

He wasn't a killer. His crime was over, and now he had to live with the consequences, yet he wasn't sure what to do. He was willing to face justice for the part he had played, yet he feared should he hand himself over, the truth would never be discovered.

A thought occurred to him as he stared at his now clean hands.

If he wanted the truth to come out in the way it needed to, he might be forced to guide the police in the proper direction, but to do so, he couldn't be running around the city dressed as he was.

He had to risk going home.

En Route to Karl Lensing Residence

Berlin, Nazi Germany

Vogel listened as Stadler relayed the results of his interviews, nothing of which sounded important. It could be that the young man asked the wrong questions, that he didn't intimidate the witnesses enough because of his young age, or could simply be that they had nothing worthwhile to say. The takeaways from their afternoon's efforts, as far as he was concerned, were that they needed to look further into this Karl individual simply to eliminate him from the suspect pool, and they needed to find out who these long-haired boys might have been, though he was equally confident they would lead nowhere, as there was no evidence they were friends of Annie's.

The real takeaway was that they needed to consider the possibility Annie's mother might have been involved in the murder. If she had found out about her daughter's clandestine rendezvous, and caught them in their post-coital bliss, the family's plans for selling her off to the wealthiest Nazi bidder with her virtue intact instead of wrecked on the bedsheets, might have been enough to put her in a rage.

It could explain the stab wounds, but could it explain the slitting of the throat that had occurred first? He had to put himself in her possible frame of mind. Any young man would have immediately left the bed and retreated into a corner when the irate mother of the woman he had just had sex with entered. It would be a natural reaction that would then give her direct access to her daughter. If she had known why she was going there, she might have brought a knife with her, or she might have taken one from the kitchen. He would have to ask Emilia Schmitt to recheck her cutlery. But if she had a knife, she might have immediately slit her daughter's throat in a cold rage to punish her for what she had done, then, after she partially regained her senses, in an emotional rage, stabbed her daughter repeatedly to punish her once again for having made her commit such a crime.

It did fit, though it didn't explain why she was tied up. Had that been some sort of sex game? Had it been done after the murder? And why didn't the boyfriend stop the mother? He might have been scared when she entered the room, but as soon as she attacked her daughter, wouldn't he have intervened?

He chewed his cheek. It wasn't a reaction that could be counted upon. Some men would leap to the young woman's defense, others would cower in fear, which might explain why they hadn't heard from him. He would know exactly who Annie's family was, and to go to the police and accuse the wife of a senior Nazi official of having murdered her own daughter in cold blood, was one sure-fire way to make certain you were never seen again. The very notion that a mother could murder her daughter in such a manner was disgusting, however he had seen worse things over his career, and for the moment, it was as good a theory as any that might explain the stray hair.

"Did you find out anything interesting?"

He snapped out of his train of thought, realizing he hadn't been listening to his partner. "What?"

"I said, did you find out anything interesting?"

"Not really."

"You look like you did."

"Huh?"

"We've been working together for over a year, and I know when there's something on your mind, and you've got something on your mind."

Vogel grunted. "You're right, I do, but it's just a wild theory right now that's not worth mentioning."

"Tell me."

"I can't. It might taint the investigation if I do, but if any more evidence comes to light that gives it some weight, you'll be the first to know."

Stadler shrugged. "Fine. So you still don't trust me."

Vogel chuckled. "Now you're getting it."

Stadler sighed. "Do you think we're going to be able to solve this one?"

Vogel glanced at him. "I have no idea. At the moment, we certainly don't seem to have any real leads, but it hasn't even been a day. Hell, it hasn't even been half a day. Something usually comes up. Most murders aren't well-planned, so mistakes are made. The placement of her personal items so close to the crime scene suggests this wasn't a well-planned murder. Somebody saw something or heard something. We just need to do the groundwork to find out who." He leaned forward and checked the street number of the apartment buildings as they drove by, then parked. "We're here."

Minutes later, they were sitting in the living room of a very humble apartment filled with dozens of dismantled devices, from radios to gramophones and more, someone obviously a tinkerer. Karl Lensing sat across from him, a knee bouncing, knuckles constantly cracked as the nervous young man looked anywhere but at either of the detectives. His parents sat silently on a couch, the young man's mother having just served tea.

"Do you know why we're here?"

Karl nodded. "I think so. It's about Miss Annie, isn't it?"

"It's about Miss Dettman, yes."

"So, it's true?"

"Yes, she's been murdered."

Karl's parents gasped, evidently not aware of what had transpired.

"How did you find out?" asked Vogel.

"Ernst called a friend of mine who has a phone, and he came by to let me know."

"And did he tell you why we might be coming to speak with you?"

If Karl could appear more nervous than before, he now did.

"You don't have to answer that. We both know why I'm here. Why don't you tell us what happened?"

Karl glanced at his mother, his cheeks flushed, then turned away, staring at the floor. "I didn't see her. I didn't look at her. I swear."

"Just tell us what happened."

"Ernst told me to prune the trees on the south side because they were getting too close to the house. So, I was on a ladder, clipping the branches, when I heard Miss Annie cry out. I turned my head and saw her standing in the window, not two feet from my face, holding a towel in front of her. I immediately closed my eyes and climbed down the ladder. She began to laugh, then I heard shouts from her mother and her father, and I heard Miss Annie telling them that nothing had happened, that she had merely been startled and that I had seen nothing, but less than an hour later, I was fired."

"And what did they say when you protested your innocence?"

"I didn't bother, sir. There was no point. Her parents are extremely protective of her and her virtue."

"Explain."

Karl glanced up at him, then at his mother. "I'm not sure I can say what I mean in present company."

Vogel smiled slightly, holding up a hand. "I know what you mean by virtue, what I mean is, why do you think they were overly protective?"

"Oh, everyone knew, sir. Her parents were interviewing young men as if auditioning them for a play. They were determined to find her a suitable husband as quickly as possible."

"And do you know if they had come to a decision?"

He shook his head. "I made it a point to avoid any interaction with them. All I know of the affair is what the other staff told me. I stuck to the outdoors as much as possible. Those people scare me."

"Those people?"

He glanced at Stadler. "Umm, forget I said that."

"You mean the Dettmans? Or do you mean the Nazis?"

Karl shrunk even more, answering the question. "I really shouldn't say."

Vogel had his answer. "Can you think of anyone that might want to harm Annie?"

Karl vigorously shook his head as he made eye contact for the first time. "No, she was wonderful, so friendly to everybody. I can't imagine anyone wanting to hurt her."

"Did you ever see any of her friends?"

He shrugged. "I'm sure I must have, but like I said, I was usually outside paying attention to my work. I never wanted to get involved in the family's business."

"Did you ever see a man with long hair?"

"Huh?"

"Did you ever see a man with long hair?"

He shook his head. "I don't think so. No one of that type would be associated with the Dettmans, I'm sure."

Vogel rose, as did the rest of the room. He handed Karl his card. "If you can think of anything that might be helpful, please let me know, day or night."

"Yes, sir."

Vogel thanked Karl's parents for their hospitality, then headed for the door. He stopped, turning to Karl. "Are you the tinkerer?"

Karl smiled uncomfortably. "Yes, sir."

"And you actually repair these things?"

His mother beamed with pride. "He can repair anything."

Vogel nodded. "Interesting."

Vogel Residence

Berlin, Nazi Germany

"So, Sofia, tell us the truth. Did you finally see my guy?"

Sofia Vogel put her tea down, regarding her friend Ingrid. Every Saturday for the better part of a decade, the same four friends had gathered for tea, alternating between residences weekly. This week it was her turn. "Your guy?"

"You know, my guy." Ingrid motioned at the sandwiches, Sofia finally clueing in.

"Oh, God, no! I would never do that!"

"Then how do you explain all this?"

"Wolfgang finally had his partner over for lunch, and he brought his day's rations with him."

"Hasn't he been working with him for over a year?" asked Elke.

"Yes, but he's a bit of an acquired taste, shall we say."

"Tell us about him."

Her friends all leaned in.

She chose her words carefully. "There's not much to tell that my husband would want repeated."

"Oh, you can tell us. Who are we going to tell?" urged Ingrid. "How often do we actually have something new to talk about?"

Sofia frowned, but as she stared at the faces of her three best friends, their eagerness clear, she gave in and sighed. "Fine. He's a young man—"

"Ooo! Handsome?"

Sofia gave Ingrid a look. "Yes, very handsome. I'm sure your husband would agree."

Elke giggled. "Speaking of things that shouldn't be repeated!"

They all laughed.

"Why doesn't your husband like him?" asked Susanne.

"Because he didn't earn the job. His father used his connections to not only keep him away from the front, but to get him assigned as a detective straight out of the academy."

Susanne shrugged. "Well, if there was anything my husband could have done to keep our son here in Berlin, I'm sure he would have done it."

"I'm sure most fathers would," agreed Elke. "Who would want to send their son to die in some foreign country?"

"Any good Nazi would," muttered Ingrid.

A silence fell over the room for a moment, Elke breaking it. "So, he's not any good at the job?"

Sofia was grateful for an end to the awkward silence. None of them were devout Nazis, though these days nobody dared express those opinions unless one truly trusted those they were with. "Not really, though that comes with experience. So, maybe eventually he will be, but he skipped the four years of being a regular police officer, where you learn how to interact with the public and how to read people. My husband always says that the key to being a good detective is being able to tell if someone's lying to you. And he learned that while walking the beat."

Elke shuddered. "I can't imagine doing what he does. Staring at dead bodies day in and day out, trying to figure out what sort of depraved person committed such an atrocity."

"Does it ever get to him?" asked Susanne.

Sofia considered her reply carefully, erring on the side of caution lest word get out her husband might be troubled, something not tolerated these days. "I'm sure he must, however he would never admit that to me. I think when he's dealing with the murder of a child or a young person, it does." She shook her head. "Let's change the subject. This is too depressing."

Ingrid held up one of the sandwiches. "Yes, let's get back to the case of this generous spread you've put out for us today. You expect us to believe that your husband's partner just happened to come here for the first time in over a year for lunch, brought his day's rations to give to a family he doesn't know, the family of a partner he doesn't get along with, mere hours before we were due to arrive?" She wagged the sandwich at her. "I think you've got a guy, and he's not mine."

Sofia batted her hand. "You're terrible. All I did was put some sandwiches together with bread that would go stale. It's no better than any of you have ever put out."

Ingrid lowered her voice, leaning toward the others. "Exactly. And we don't have husbands with generous partners, well connected in the Nazi Party."

Another series of giggles.

Ingrid finished off her sandwich in three bites. Everyone was now leaning back comfortably, their appetites satisfied, their tea almost finished. Ingrid checked the clock sitting on the mantle.

"Oh dear, is that the time? I must be going. I have to get dinner ready. My in-laws are coming over tonight."

Everyone rose and minutes later, Sofia's friends were gone for another week. She frowned at the leftovers, her attempt to impress having succeeded, and having resulted in waste.

She smiled.

"Children! There are some sandwiches out here!"

Little feet hammered on the floor, and every crumb of what remained was inhaled.

As she cleaned up, she was left to wonder whether her friends believed Stadler had indeed brought her family this extra bounty, and the more she thought of it, the more she regretted putting on her display.

She growled.

I'm not going to feel guilty.

She had done nothing wrong, merely sharing her good fortune with friends. Yet these were friends who broke the law by participating in the black market, though they were good people, otherwise she wouldn't associate with them. Everyone was desperate these days to bring a little bit of normalcy back to their life. Almost everyone she knew had "a guy," someone to go to when they needed something not available in the stores, some little extra beyond what the government rations provided.

But no matter how tempted she was, she could never take part in that segment of German society. Her husband's job meant everything. It meant security for her and the children, and it meant respect.

And it was a career that kept him from the front.

If he were to lose his job as a policeman, he would either be forced into the *Wehrmacht*, the Army, or worse, since he was technically a member of the SS, into their ranks, where he'd be forced to commit untold atrocities.

She stared at the plates as she washed them, cursing at herself for having done what she did, and prayed her friends didn't start any rumors that might risk all their futures.

En Route to the Adi Dassler Shoe Factory

Berlin, Nazi Germany

"You know what I'm afraid of?"

Vogel glanced at his partner. "What?"

"That the stray hair is just that, a stray. It has nothing to do with the murder, and it's distracting us."

Vogel parked in front of the shoe factory. "It's a definite possibility. This wouldn't be the first time an investigation had been led astray by a red herring. But, unfortunately, we can't dismiss it outright. We have to keep pursuing the investigation in all directions, and eventually we'll either rule it out or we'll rule it in." He turned off the engine. "This is where I think we can make some serious progress."

"You think her friends are going to know who the boy was that she was meeting?"

"I think at least one of them absolutely knows. The question is, are they going to be willing to tell us?"

Vogel climbed out of the car and the factory manager, Martin Teufel, greeted them.

"Gentlemen, I have everything ready for you. The girls you asked to be brought down are all here, and I've set aside a room for you."

"Thank you very much, sir," said Vogel, shaking the man's hand. "We appreciate the effort you've gone to."

"Oh, I'd do anything to help you find Annie's killer. She was such a hard worker, so good to everyone, despite the fact she didn't have to be here. Most of the girls like her are only here for show, to make their fathers look good. Annie actually enjoyed the work and did it well, and insisted she never be treated any differently from the others. She put in her hours, took only the breaks she was entitled to, and never used her father's position to get out of doing any of the less desirable aspects of the job."

"Yet there's always someone you can't get along with, isn't there?"

Teufel shifted uncomfortably. "Well, I suppose."

"And who was it that she didn't get along with?"

"There was one, another daughter of a senior Party official."

"Her name?"

"Frieda Brack."

"Is she here today?"

He laughed. "On a weekend? No, you'll never see any of them here on a weekend, except for Annie if needed."

"Was Annie due to work today?"

"No, this was her weekend off. She wasn't due back until Monday."

"Do you have any men working here?"

"Of course. None, however, fit for the front. Mostly men in their fifties and sixties like me, others wounded from the World War. It's mostly women here, though."

"Any of these men have eyes for Annie?"

"All of them had eyes for her. She is one of the most beautiful women I've ever seen. But if you're asking would any of them have acted on it, I doubt it. Like I said, most of the people here are triple her age, the rest incapable of satisfying a woman like her. And besides, everyone knew who her father was."

"All right, we'll start interviewing her friends now, but I'll need you to get me the contact details for Miss Brack."

"Yes, sir." He showed them to an outer office where three young women sat in chairs along the far wall. They all leaped to their feet the moment their boss entered. "Ladies, this is Kriminalinspektor Vogel and his partner Kriminalassistent Stadler."

They all bowed their heads slightly, all clearly distraught and nervous.

"Is it true, sir? Is Annie dead?" asked one of them.

Vogel nodded. "I'm afraid so."

Cries and sobs erupted and all three of them clung to each other.

"Enough of that, girls, enough of that," said Teufel. "These men have a job to do, and the sooner they get it done, the sooner you can get home to your families, and the sooner they can get on with catching Annie's killer."

The women separated and Vogel picked a brunette. "Your name is?"

"Angelika Catel."

"Very well, Miss Catel, let's start with you, shall we?"

"Yes, sir."

Teufel showed them to an office and Angelika sat on one side of the table, Vogel across from her, with Stadler standing in the corner behind her. Vogel jotted her name down on his pad along with the date and time.

"So, how long have you known Annie?"

"Almost a year, I guess."

"And how did you meet her?"

"When she started working here."

"And you're friends?"

"Yes, I hope so. At least, I guess we were, if she's dead." The young woman's lip trembled as she struggled to maintain control.

"When was the last time you saw her?"

"Friday, on the factory floor."

"Did she say where she was going? Did she have any plans?"

"No, I don't think so, at least I don't recall. A few of us were going out for drinks after work. I remember asking Monika where Annie was, and she said she asked her if she wanted to come but Annie said she wasn't feeling well. Monika might know more, but I'm sorry, I don't."

"Did Annie have a boyfriend?"

The young woman giggled. "Annie? A boyfriend? No, her father never would have allowed it. From what Annie told me, her father planned to marry her off to the highest bidder in the Nazi Party."

Stadler's eyebrows rose in the corner at the blunt statement. Vogel didn't react visibly. "She actually told you that?"

"Yes, though it was in the strictest of confidence one night." She frowned. "I suppose that doesn't matter anymore now, does it?"

"No, it doesn't. Anything she told you in confidence, you should tell me, because it may lead to her killer."

She shivered at the word. "Do you think she was murdered by someone she knew? Or maybe she was murdered because of who her father is?"

"I can't discuss such details. Can you think of anyone who might want to harm her?"

She vigorously shook her head. "Oh, no, not Annie. Everybody loved her."

"There were no secret jealousies?"

"I don't think so." She smirked slightly. "And they'd be secret, so…"

Vogel smiled. "What about Frieda Brack?"

Her eyes widened at the mention of the name. "Oh my, I forgot about her. Yes, her and Annie didn't get along, or rather, she didn't get along with Annie. Annie never took the bait when goaded. She would either just walk away or smile pleasantly. She was just a wonderful person. I never heard her raise her voice, or say anything out of anger, or anything untoward about anyone. But Frieda, she's a piece of work. She seems to hate everyone and everything, and resents being here every moment she is. I think she was probably annoyed at how Annie seemed to be happy about working here, toiling day in and day out when she didn't have to."

"So, Annie didn't have a boyfriend. Did she ever mention finding anyone attractive, interesting, intriguing?"

"Oh, when we'd be out, she might point out a cute boy, but she never acted on it. She knew there was never any future if she were to bring someone home to meet her parents. Her father would probably have flogged her."

Vogel's eyebrows ticked up. "Did he beat her?"

"Oh, no! It's just an expression. If anyone were to beat her, it would have been her mother."

"You said that Annie didn't join you for drinks last night?"

"That's right."

"Did she normally join you?"

"Yes. The five of us would go out together almost every Friday."

"Five?"

She gestured toward the door leading to the hallway where her two friends were. "The three of us, Annie, and Petra Berkner."

"Right. Is this the first time she canceled, or has she been canceling a lot lately?"

She shrugged. "We all miss a Friday here or there. One of us will have family plans or isn't feeling well or is just too tired. She might have canceled once or twice in the past month or two. Nothing really stands out."

"Now, you said she didn't express any interest in anyone, but is there anyone you can think of who was interested in her?"

She laughed. "Oh, everyone was interested in her. Not only was she gorgeous, but she came from a good family. Her father is very high up in the Nazi Party." She smiled sheepishly. "But I suppose you already know that."

"Yes, we do."

"Then you know how much of a catch she is. Any young man who won her would not only have a beautiful and friendly wife, he would have a secure future in the Reich."

"Does anyone, in particular, come to mind?"

She shook her head. "Not really. With her father the way he was, no one would act on their desires. They might smile at her and stare at her, but unless she reciprocated, I don't think any of them would dare make a move for fear of her father."

Vogel flipped back in his notes. "There was a party several months ago at Dieter Maier's house. Annie was there. Do you recall that event?"

Her face brightened. "Yes, that was the best party I think since the war began. It was like the good old days. Annie was invited because of who she was, and she invited all of us. It was quite the event. It was the sons and daughters of the who's who. There were more blondes and fake blondes there than I've ever seen in one place." She giggled.

"Can you tell me about the host?"

"I don't know much about him. His father's very high in the Party, that's about all I know. I was introduced to him during the evening, but beyond the standard greetings, nothing was really said."

"And did he express any interest in Annie?"

"No more than anyone else." Her eyes widened slightly, and a finger raised from her lap. "There was one boy that was there, though, that I remember speaking with Annie for quite some time. It was toward the end of the night, so I was a little tipsy."

"Do you know his name?"

She shook her head "No, I had never seen him before."

"Did you get the impression that Annie knew him?"

"When I noticed them speaking, they seemed to be quite comfortable with each other, though I don't know how long they had been speaking before I noticed. I really can't say."

"Did you ask her about him?"

"To be perfectly honest, I had forgotten about it until just now. Like I said, it was quite the party, and my memory is fuzzy toward the end." She giggled. "I'm not even sure how I got home."

"Can you describe him?"

She shook her head. "I'm sorry, like I said, my memory—"

"Is fuzzy," finished Vogel. She giggled. He handed her his card. "If you think of anything, call day or night."

"Yes, sir."

He rose. "Please send in Monika."

"Yes, sir." She stood and left, Vogel closing the door behind her.

Stadler stared at him. "Do you think we might have just got our first lead?"

Vogel tilted his head to the side. "Possibly. We definitely need to find out who she was talking to at that party. That suggests there was indeed a boyfriend, and he met her at Dieter Maier's party several months ago."

There was a tentative knock at the door and Vogel opened it to find another young woman standing there. He smiled, attempting to put her at ease as he held his hand out. "Please, take a seat."

She sat and he quickly went through the routine questions. The young woman had met Annie a year ago when she had started working at the factory, considered her a friend, they regularly went out on Friday nights, could think of no one beyond Frieda who didn't get along with her, and confirmed Annie had no boyfriend of whom she was aware.

Her answers were almost identical to her predecessor's.

"Do you remember a party several months ago, at Dieter Maier's house?"

"Oh, do I! That was the most exciting night of my life. I felt so…so…so rich! It was such a beautiful home, all kinds of food and drink, everyone was dressed so beautifully. I wasn't sure I wanted to go. I just knew I wouldn't fit in, but Annie lent us all dresses. She has such fine clothes. Such a lucky girl." Her face sagged. "I'm sorry, I guess I shouldn't have said that. I suppose she wasn't lucky after all."

"Do you remember Annie interacting with anyone in particular?"

Her eyes narrowed at the question. "I don't think so."

"She wasn't speaking with a young man toward the end of the evening?"

Her jaw dropped. "Oh my God, I forgot about that! It was quite the evening, so I think I had one too many drinks, but yes, I remember that now. She was speaking to a young man for quite some time and seemed very interested in him, which was unusual for her. Her father was quite the beast with grand plans for her."

Vogel played dumb. "What do you mean?"

"He intended to marry her off to secure his future. Can you imagine such a thing? To force your daughter to marry someone she didn't love, because you were concerned one day you might lose your job?" She shuddered. "Disgusting."

"Did she ever mention that her father had any particular person in mind?"

She shook her head. "No, though she did confide in me a few weeks ago that she feared her father did have something in the works, and that she might be forcibly engaged soon."

"How did she feel about that?"

"Horrible."

"Back to this young man she met at the party. Do you know who he was?"

She shook her head. "No, I'd never seen him before."

"Have you seen him since?"

"No, I don't think so, but then again, like I said, my memory is a little unclear."

"What did he look like?"

"I'm not sure, like I said—"

Vogel held out a hand. "I know, I know. But let's speak in generalities. Tall, short?"

She shrugged. "Average height. But he was across the room, so I can't be sure."

"Was he taller than Annie, or shorter?"

"Oh, definitely taller." Her eyes flared. "I'd say a good head taller because he was looking down as they spoke."

"What color hair?"

"Brown, I think. Maybe black."

"Short? Long?"

"Huh?"

"The hair."

"Short, of course. None of those types would be welcome at a party like that."

"Slim, husky?"

"Slim, very fit from what I remember. I do seem to remember thinking he was quite fetching."

"Do you remember what he was wearing?"

"It was formal attire. Most of the young men were in their dress uniforms."

"And this man?"

"I know he was dressed in black. I think it might have been an SS uniform, or it might have simply been a tuxedo. I just can't remember, I'm sorry."

"What did she think of the SS?"

She shifted in her chair. "I'm sure I don't know."

Vogel smiled slightly. "From what you know of her opinion of the SS, can you see her talking to one for so long and so pleasantly, if she didn't know him from before?"

A firm head shake. "No, now that you mention it, I can't imagine her giving the time of day to a member of the SS. She would be polite, of course, because it isn't wise not to be, but she certainly wouldn't voluntarily carry on a conversation with someone like that."

"Is there anything else you can tell me about this young man? Light-skinned, tanned?"

She shook her head. "No, I'm sorry."

"Were they drinking?"

"I assume so, though Annie was never much of a drinker. She was always scared of what her parents would think about anything she did, so she always kept herself under control."

"Had you noticed anything odd in her behavior lately? Apparently, she canceled plans with you and your friends last night?"

"Oh, yes, that was nothing. She just said she wasn't feeling well, so was going to go home." Her eyes widened. "But she didn't go home, did she?" She squinted. "Or was she murdered at home?"

Vogel shook his head. "No, she wasn't murdered at home."

She gasped. "She lied to me!" She pursed her lips. "Or her plans changed. Maybe she started to feel better and decided to go out." Another gasp, her hand darting to her mouth. "Was she coming to join us and then someone killed her?"

"That will all come out in our investigation." He handed her his card. "If you think of anything, please contact me, day or night. Please send the last one in."

She left the room and Vogel held the door shut. Stadler remained leaning in the corner, his arms folded.

"Do you really think it could be an SS member that we're looking for?"

Vogel shrugged. "It's possible. Someone like that would certainly be capable of cold-blooded murder. I think, however, that if she had misgivings about the SS, she wouldn't participate in a conversation for that long."

"One doesn't reject the SS too quickly."

"The average person doesn't, no. However, all she would have to do is mention who her father was, and the young man would salute and walk away. A young SS officer isn't going to risk his career over a hopeless cause that could end it."

There was a knock at the door and Vogel opened it, the final young woman standing there. He invited her in and she took a seat. She put a lunch pail on the table beside her and his eyes narrowed, not having noticed anyone carrying one when they arrived.

"Where did you get that?"

She glanced at it. "Oh, I left it here yesterday because we went out for drinks immediately after work. I figured I'd grab it out of my locker since I was here."

"Do you all have lockers?"

"Yes." He glanced at Stadler and jerked his head toward the door. "Get me the contents of Annie's."

"Yes, sir." Stadler left the room and Vogel continued the interrogation, finding nothing new beyond the fact that this one, Katrin Kimm, was certain the man was in a simple dark suit, not an SS uniform, and had short brown hair. She also gave an exact date for the party.

Saturday, March 15th.

"Did you talk to her about the boy she met?"

"Not that night, but I did talk to her on Monday when she came into work."

Vogel sat up a little straighter. "And what did she say?"

Katrin shrugged. "Nothing much. She didn't seem comfortable talking about him, and I guess that makes sense considering her father wouldn't approve."

Again he played dumb. "Why wouldn't he approve?"

"Well, I'm sure the others told you he had plans to marry her off to some rich old Nazi."

He played a hunch. "Yes, but there's something else isn't there."

She stared at her hands wringing in her lap. "Well, I really shouldn't be talking out of turn."

"Miss, Annie is dead. If you know anything that can help us find out who her murderer was, you have to tell me. You won't be betraying her, you'll be fighting for her."

She drew a deep breath and held it before sighing heavily. "You're right, of course. She didn't tell me much, but she did say he was an old friend that she hadn't seen in a long time."

His heart rate picked up a few extra beats. "Did she say what his name was?"

"No."

"Did she say where she knew him from?"

"No."

"Any indication of how long ago it was since she had last seen him?"

"No, nothing. She said he was an old friend and to please not ask her any more questions, so I respected her wishes."

"Had you seen this young man before anywhere?"

"No."

"Since?"

"No."

"And after this party, was Annie acting any differently?"

A slight smile crept up the corners of her mouth. "Actually, now that you mention it, she did seem a little happier for a while, until a couple of weeks ago when she told us she feared her father might be close to making a decision."

"And did she say who he had decided upon?"

"No, I don't think she knew, though her father seemed quite pleased."

Stadler entered the room and returned to his position in the corner, excitement on his face. Vogel handed her his card. "If you think of anything else, call me day or night." She took the card and left the room. Vogel closed the door.

"You're not going to believe what I found in her locker."

"What?"

Stadler held up a bound notebook.

"What's that?"

"Her diary."

Luft Family Grocery

Berlin, Nazi Germany

Ingrid peered into the bag and smiled. "Did you manage to get everything?"

"Yes, ma'am. Everything on your list."

She closed up the bag. "That's wonderful. Perhaps I'll be able to escape my mother-in-law's scathing reviews of my cooking."

Her grocer and "guy," Manfred Luft, laughed heartily. "Anyone who complains about a dinner made from these ingredients is merely doing so because they like the sound of their own voice."

She patted the bag. "This is why I'm always telling my friend she should come to you. Her life would be so much easier, though she never will."

"Well, if she changes her mind, you know where to find me."

"Oh, her husband's a police officer. She'll never be changing her mind, though the spread she put on today for tea certainly had me wondering."

Luft paused. "Do you mean Mrs. Vogel?"

Ingrid's hand darted to her chest as she inhaled quickly. "How could you possibly know that?"

He shrugged. "It's my business to know my customers. Mrs. Vogel shops here, and you've mentioned her several times in reference to your afternoon teas."

Ingrid sighed with relief. "Yes, of course, of course."

He eyed her for a moment. "What made you think she had finally broken down?"

"Oh, she had some extra rations that she shared with us today. She said they came from her husband's new partner. I gave her a bit of a hard time about it just for fun. I'm sure she was telling us the truth, though you never know, her husband *is* a police officer." She winked. "Maybe they're conducting an investigation!"

Luft regarded her, his tone muted. "Yes, perhaps."

Her chest tightened and her heart hammered as she realized she had said too much. She wagged her hand in front of her. "Please ignore what I just said. I'm positive it was all innocent and there's nothing to concern yourself about."

"I'm sure you're right."

She bowed her head slightly. "Until next time."

He smiled broadly. "Until next time. Good luck with your dinner tonight."

"Thank you."

She hurried out the back entrance to the grocery and down the alleyway then out onto the main street, her mind guiding her automatically as her thoughts were consumed with what had just happened. She cursed at herself repeatedly for her habit of talking far too much. Yes, she had known Luft for years, though they weren't friends. He was merely her local grocer. They were on friendly terms, but family secrets should never be shared. Casual exchanges about the weather or the season were all that should be expected.

Instead, this man knew who her friends were, what their husbands did, and now, because of her loose lips, might actually believe Sofia's husband was investigating the black market.

She growled, causing several people waiting for the tram to back away. She flashed a smile. "Sorry, bad day."

There were several murmurs of understanding. There were a lot of bad days for everyone, and each day seemed a little worse. With the bombings they were experiencing, she couldn't believe the war was going the way the leadership had expected. It seemed like every week, more goods were being rationed. Soldiers needed to be fed if they were to win this fight, and she understood that, and was willing to make a sacrifice.

They all were.

After all, they were their husbands, brothers, sons. There wasn't a person here who didn't have someone they knew serving, someone they knew wounded or killed. And England wasn't even defeated yet. Everything she had read and heard suggested England was on its knees and would soon capitulate. And once that happened, Germany could turn its attention to the other fronts in this war. Without England as a staging area, there was no risk on the Atlantic Coast.

At least that's what the radio told her.

She boarded the tram and took a seat, clutching her black market goods to her chest, wondering whether she should warn Sofia about what had just happened. She stared at the bag handed to her by a man she had known for years. She couldn't imagine Luft doing anything violent. He was a good man. She knew his wife who worked with him, who fondly spoke of their three children, including two boys serving in Poland. He was a family man, and she couldn't imagine him doing anything untoward, yet the proof he was a criminal was in her arms at this very moment.

He participated in the black market.

And that was a crime.

If he were caught, he would be imprisoned and perhaps even executed. But wasn't it too late? She had already said what she said. If Luft had his suspicions about Sofia's husband, then those seeds were already planted, and nothing could be done about it now. If she revealed what she had said, and then something were to happen to her friend, everyone would blame her, and her life would be ruined, her family's as well.

No one would risk speaking around her.

She could lose all of her friends and what limited social standing she possessed. She closed her eyes, the debate raging, and in the end, a decision was made.

The only thing that mattered was her friend's safety.

Bile filled her mouth at the thought of something happening to Sofia or her family. She sighed. Tomorrow, after church, she would tell her friend about her indiscretion, and then face the consequences, should there be any.

Dettman Residence

Berlin, Nazi Germany

Hermann Dettman sat in his home office, his chest tight, his pulse pounding in his ears as his stomach churned. He gripped the framed photo of his daughter, taken on her sixteenth birthday.

Such a good girl.

She was his princess, and all he had ever wanted was the best for her. They were not a wealthy family. They had never had any power or influence. All they had had was the good fortune of the Führer and his National Socialist German Workers Party frequently meeting in the beerhall near his home in Munich. It was his favorite watering hole, and he had heard them railing against the government, night in and night out.

And then one night he had asked if he could join them.

They had eagerly agreed, as they were desperate for new converts. And in short order, he was a trusted member of the fledgling Nazi Party, membership number 952. The Führer was number 555, with the numbering starting at 500 to make it appear in those early days as if they had more followers.

He was one of the originals.

For the most part, he had agreed with what they were saying. He believed in their cause to return Germany to its former glory, and at first, had gained nothing beyond a group of loyal friends. But once the Party became something more, and finally took power, he was rewarded. He now lived in a grand house, and had lots of money, though was by no means rich. He had an important job that gave him a great amount of influence, far more than what he would have had had he not joined them at their table that first night.

His greatest fear was that he would offend the wrong person, that he would fail in his job, and that they would lose everything. His daughter was only nineteen, but her teenage years had been spent living very well, and he couldn't stand to see her impoverished once again. Not to mention his wife, who had taken to this lifestyle with gusto. If they ever lost what they now had, he feared what she would do. He was well aware his daughter hadn't been happy with his plans to arrange a marriage for her. It wasn't typically done in today's Germany, however it wasn't unheard of among senior Nazi families in an attempt to keep the race pure, and bear the next generation that would lead the Thousand-Year Reich after its founders were dead and gone.

It was why he had taken great care in selecting the right partner. The young man would come from a good Nazi family, of course, but also one that had wealth, so that should their status change for the worse, their daughter would be provided for, and perhaps through her, they would still maintain a healthy lifestyle.

But the man also had to be someone his daughter could learn to love. It was why he had rejected so many offers, and why he hadn't considered anyone over the age of thirty. The idea of some old man pawing at his princess sickened him.

He pulled the file from his drawer for the young man he had decided upon, and opened it, staring at the photo. He was a fine-looking man, and he had met him several times along with his parents. Annie had met him as well a couple of weeks ago, though hadn't been aware as to why. He would have made a good match, but none of that mattered now.

He put down the photo of his daughter, his shoulders shaking, his reason to live gone. All he had worked for, all he had accomplished, had been for his family, but it held no meaning anymore.

His family had been destroyed.

There was a knock at the door and his wife entered. "The staff didn't want to disturb you, but they need to know if you're having dinner."

He sighed, leaning back. "I'm not very hungry, though I suppose I should eat something. How are you doing?"

She shrugged. "As good as can be expected, I suppose. It's hard not to blame her."

His eyes shot wide. "What the hell is that supposed to mean?"

"You know exactly what I mean. She was supposed to be out with friends. She lied to us."

His wife was right, however to blame the victim was ridiculous. "She was young, but she was an adult, and was free to do what she wanted with her life."

"That's nonsense and you know it, otherwise you wouldn't have been arranging a marriage for her."

He frowned. "I was doing what was best for her."

"You keep telling yourself that. If you hadn't been so busy trying to marry her off to some rich Nazi, maybe she wouldn't have been sneaking around, having clandestine affairs with men before she was married."

"So, now it's my fault? Make up your mind, woman. Maybe it's your fault because you enjoy this new life we have too much, and I've been busy trying to make sure you never have to go back to living the way we used to."

She glared at him. "Don't go pretending you don't love it as much as I do."

His heart raced as a little bit of truth was about to be revealed. "I may enjoy our new standard of living, however don't for a moment believe I think it was worth the soul I was forced to sacrifice."

The anger in her face relaxed slightly. "What do you mean?"

He waved a hand at their surroundings, at their existence. "We were never meant for this. This was never meant to be our life. Before the Party, life was hard, but we were happy. We had a home, we had our daughter, we were fed. Nothing was easy, but don't you remember those nights, the three of us curled up in bed, reading a book aloud to each other, all the laughter and the smiles?"

"I think you're forgetting how hard things actually were."

He shook his head. "No, I'm not. Yes, during the Depression things were horrible, but they were horrible for everyone. Yet we managed. In the new Germany, things have improved for everyone. We would be enjoying those benefits even if we weren't members of the Party with some rich Jew's house. Don't you ever wonder where the owners of this house went?"

She shrugged. "It never occurred to me to think about it."

"Well, think about it. Maybe you'll feel a little bit differently the next time you stare at it thinking it's yours. It can be taken away from us just as easily as it was taken away from the previous owners. And now our daughter's gone, we're too old to have another, and the world we live in means we are one offense away from losing it all. And the safety net we thought we were going to have by securing Annie's future…" His voice cracked.

His wife sat across from him, her chin on her chest as her tears flowed. "That future was gone the moment she had sex with that boy."

He eyed her. "What boy?"

She looked up at him. "What?"

"What boy? You said, 'as soon as she had sex with that boy.'"

She batted her hand. "I just mean, it was obviously a boy she had sex with. No one in particular."

"Oh."

"As soon as she lost her virginity, she lost her value. You know how these people are. They want their son marrying someone pure so that they can start populating their great race."

He frowned. His wife was right. The Party was obsessed with repopulation, and that repopulation had to be pure. The *Lebensraum* program had been embraced and expanded by the Nazis with the Lebensborn program. The World War had been devastating on the male population of Germany, triggering a precipitous decline in the overall population. For Germany to succeed, the Fatherland required a large, robust, pure next generation to provide the fighting men of tomorrow. Arranged marriages, the banning of birth control, women encouraged to have unwanted babies that would then be taken care of by the state, impregnation of women in conquered territories by German soldiers, and any other policy that might increase the birthrate of pure Aryan children, was already in practice or being considered.

And Annie losing her virginity would have changed her perceived worth, though more likely in the eyes of the mothers of the future in-laws than of the man she would marry. Today's youth were far more promiscuous than in his day.

She stared at him. "What do we do now?"

"We try to move on with our lives, honor her memory, and do whatever it takes to bring her murderer to justice."

His wife shifted in her seat. "And will we lose everything?"

He stared at her. "Would that be such a bad thing?"

His wife's shoulders slumped as she stared at her hands. "Compared to this misery, I suppose not. Without our daughter to offer to the Party, you'll need to be very careful. I've already lost my daughter. I can't lose my husband because he offends the wrong person."

His stomach churned at her words, for she was right. Their daughter married into a wealthy, well-connected family provided not only a financial safety net, but the protection of her family who might help him should he run afoul of the Party, as they wouldn't want their daughter-in-law associated with anything untoward, and by extension, her new family, should he do something wrong. Now with her gone, everything was on his shoulders.

And the tremendous pressure he had faced for years had just grown tenfold.

Wilhelmine Ring Residential District

Berlin, Nazi Germany

He entered his family's apartment building through the rear alley. He pressed his ear against the door to the stairwell and listened for footfalls, but heard none. He hurried up the three flights of stairs to the floor that had been their home since they arrived six months ago. He hadn't wanted to come, though he had no real choice. His asthma prevented him from joining the military, and his employment options were limited. His father had picked up the entire family and moved it from Munich to Berlin for a new job and better prospects. Yet it had just been a pretense to save the family's reputation.

Something was wrong with his mother.

What, he had never been sure, his family not big on sharing, and as a result, he rarely knew what was actually happening behind the forced smiles. It wasn't that it was an unhappy household, it was that when something was wrong, he was kept in the dark. That might have been wise when he was younger, but not now that he was an adult.

His mother had never been the same since his sister Gabriele had drowned six years ago. How she had made it to the river, no one knew. He had been told it was an accident. No one was to blame, though his mother blamed herself. She had become withdrawn, even more uncommunicative than she usually was. It had been so long ago in his young life, that if it weren't for the photos still prominently displayed throughout the apartment, he would have long forgotten how his baby sister had looked.

And now his family was shattered once again.

They just weren't aware of it yet.

His father would be devastated when he found out what had happened last night, for once the truth was revealed, there would be nothing left but the photographs, and they would eventually fade as the memories had.

He pressed his ear against the apartment door, hearing nothing. He turned the handle slowly and pressed against the door, inching it open. He could hear the radio playing. It meant his father should be asleep in his chair, with his mother in the bedroom doing whatever it was she did while sequestered from the family. He stepped inside and closed the door, then tip-toed down the front hallway. As expected, his father was in his chair, his head lolled to the side, sound asleep.

He didn't envy the man. His mother was a difficult woman to live with. He was certain his father had taken a new job in an unfamiliar city to escape the memories. He recalled the argument when they were unpacking, about how many photos of his sister she was putting up. His father had wanted one family photo on the mantel, and that was it, but he had lost the argument, and now, dozens of photos were spread throughout the apartment, prompting questions every time someone would visit, for no one in Berlin knew that Gabriele was dead.

He continued past his father and successfully made it to his bedroom where he stripped out of his clothes and donned more appropriate casual attire. He grabbed his modest stash of cash he had hidden, tucked inside a copy of Jules Verne's Twenty Thousand Leagues Under the Sea. He checked himself in the mirror. His face needed to be washed and his hair combed, but he couldn't risk heading for the bathroom, as it would take him past his parents' bedroom, and an encounter with his mother was out of the question.

He successfully made it once again past his father, then as he reached for the doorknob, the floorboards creaked behind him.

"Just where do you think you're going?"

He cringed at his mother's voice. He couldn't look at her—he didn't know how he'd react. His heart was hammering now, his stomach churning, his mouth gone dry. The very sound of her voice had a combination of terror, guilt, and revulsion flowing through him. He was ashamed and disgusted with himself, and with her.

He opened the door and stepped into the hall.

"You get back inside here right now. We need to talk."

He shook his head, still not turning to face her. "I have nothing to say."

"We need to speak about what happened."

He shook his head. "No."

He closed the door then sprinted down the hall to the stairwell. The door opened behind him, but his mother said nothing, and she wouldn't, for then the neighbors might know their business. Yet the encounter had him wondering what she could possibly want to speak to him about, as she rarely volunteered any information.

And it had him worried if there was some new horror of which he wasn't yet aware, last night's revelation already shaking him to his core.

Vogel Residence

Berlin, Nazi Germany

Vogel sat in his chair, sipping his tea as his wife's knitting needles clicked away across from him. Dinner was done, a little more generous than usual thanks to Stadler's kindness at lunch. The young man was coming around, and now that Vogel knew a little more about Stadler's background, he found his opinion softening. But he wasn't ready to fully embrace him as his partner. It would take years before the trust he had shared with his last partner could be forged.

And even if that bond were formed, he would constantly be on his guard due to his underling's father's position. All that had been revealed was that young Stadler knew he shouldn't be in the position he was, and was aware that his fellow Kripo felt the same way. It didn't change the fact he had grown up in the Hitler Youth, was the son of a devout, vicious Nazi, and had been thoroughly indoctrinated into the fold. Vogel would always have to mind his tongue, and that wasn't something he looked forward to, his job difficult enough as it was. His hope now was that if he could train Stadler to be a good detective, then perhaps, he might convince the powers that be that Stadler should be a senior detective with his own junior partner to train.

Merely planting the seed would have Stadler's father placing the phone call, and the promotion would be his son's in a matter of days. It would once again mean the young man was passing fellow officers merely because of family connections, however—and Vogel was aware the very notion was selfish—why should he suffer? He deserved a real, qualified partner, though he refused to put the reputation of the force at risk by allowing Stadler to be promoted unqualified yet again. But no matter how much his underling might improve, it would still be years before Vogel would feel remotely comfortable putting the idea forward.

He returned his attention to the task at hand, resigning himself to his situation, and soon finished the last page of the diary dated a week ago. He snapped it shut, closing his eyes.

The clicking stopped. "Well?"

"Well what?"

"Did you discover anything of interest?"

"I did."

"Can you talk about it?"

"Nothing I say gets repeated to your friends."

"I'm not the gossip of the group."

"Uh-huh." He opened his eyes and waved the diary. "It looks like she started this just before we think she met her lover."

"Does she say his name?"

"No, she only gives an initial A, and she specifically says that she'll only reference him by the initial in case anyone finds her diary."

"What does she talk about?"

"Almost exclusively about how she doesn't want to marry someone she doesn't love, and how every young man she's introduced to by her father's friends sickens her. She clearly hates the Nazi regime, though appears to be patriotic enough."

"So her lover 'A,' does she say she met him at the party?"

He nodded. "Yes, at Dieter Maier's party."

"Does she mention the date?"

He shook his head. "No, but her first mention of him is the day after, so I'm going to assume it's one and the same, after all, how many parties can one person have during a war, let alone a couple of weeks?"

"Does she give any details about him that might help you track him down?"

"There was one line that said she hadn't expected to ever see him again after leaving Munich, so that makes me think they were childhood friends. That might help narrow down the list, assuming her parents are cooperative."

"Do you think they will be?"

He frowned. "I'm not sure. If they want to get at the truth no matter the consequences, then yes."

"You think they wouldn't?"

"These are different times. If the truth leads to a powerful family, it can mean the end of yours, even if you weren't in the wrong. And then there's another possibility far more disturbing…"

She eyed him as his voice drifted off. "Well, you can't say something like that and just leave it. What do you mean?"

He waved a hand in front of him. "I shouldn't have said anything. Forget it."

"Very well."

She wasn't pleased, but she was aware he shouldn't be discussing any cases with her in any capacity. He held up the diary. "One thing that this does confirm, however, is that the man she was meeting for her romantic tryst is this 'A' person. If we identify him, then we'll either have our murderer, or someone who might have witnessed the murder."

She shuddered. "I can't imagine being killed by the man you loved, and that you thought loved you."

He frowned. "It doesn't really make sense, does it? But I've seen far stranger things in my day."

She regarded him. "I suppose you have, haven't you? It never ceases to amaze me how you're able to stay sane with what you see every day."

He smiled, reaching out and patting her knee. "You and the children keep me grounded." He yawned and held up the diary along with the notes he had been taking. "I think I'm going to call it a night. I have a full day already tomorrow. We're going to be meeting with Dieter Maier and his father to see if we can identify the boy Annie was seen talking to, obviously this 'A' character, and then I'm going to have to meet with her parents once again to see if they can identify him."

She put down her knitting and smirked. "Do you mind if I join you?"

He eyed her. "Don't get any ideas, woman, I'm exhausted."

She grinned. "You just lie there. I have to burn off all this extra energy. I haven't felt this good in years. I think it's because of your young partner."

His eyes shot wide. "Excuse me?"

"The food, dear, the food."

He relaxed. "For a minute there, I thought I was going to have to go and shoot somebody."

She giggled. "I'm happy to see I can still make you jealous."

"Insanely." He wiggled his eyes. "Shall we?"

Kriminalpolizei Headquarters

Prinz-Albrecht Straße, Berlin, Nazi Germany

Vogel had a spring in his step as he entered headquarters. His wife was so good to him, that sometimes he found he took her for granted. These were difficult times, and he often forgot life must be difficult for her as well, staying at home, taking care of the children, and dealing with the fear of living in the capital of a country at war, surrounded by rabid Nazis with no concern for the law. She was shielded somewhat from the day-to-day travails by his position, but he dealt day in and day out with murder, and was quite aware what desperate people were capable of, and that things were only getting worse.

The fact the bombings so deep within Germany were increasing in regularity had to mean, despite Goebbels' broadcasts to the contrary, that the war wasn't going as well as the leadership would have the populace believe. All the Allies had to do was hold out long enough to rearm and reequip. And if the Americans ever became involved, Hitler's forays outside of Germany's borders would be swiftly brought to a halt.

And if Germans thought the Treaty of Versailles was unfair, he could only imagine what the victors would do the second time around.

He walked into the detective pool, a hail of good mornings exchanged as he strode to his desk. Stadler came over with a fresh cup of coffee and placed it in front of him. "You look like you're in a good mood."

Vogel realized he still had a smile plastered on his face. "I suppose I am."

Stadler grinned, punching him in the arm. "I think somebody had a little fun last night."

Vogel gave him the stink eye. "And I think somebody needs to mind his own business."

Stadler laughed, returning to his desk opposite his partner. He picked up a sheaf of papers. "Did you read this?"

"If that's the diary, then yes. I assume you did."

"Of course. I think I read it five times. Incredible insight into the mind of a young woman. I had no idea."

Vogel grunted. "If it's typical, I'm terrified of what I have ahead of me with my own."

Stadler shook his head. "I don't think you have anything to worry about. You and your wife are normal. These Dettmans are another matter." He shook the pages again. "This, this is a condemnation of arranged marriages. This poor girl was terrified of what was to be her future."

Vogel had to agree. "Any takeaways?"

Stadler leaned back, folding his arms. "Well, she was definitely convinced that her father had come to some decision, or was about to, so we should ask him about that."

"Agreed. What else?"

"We need to figure out who this 'A' character is. It's obviously someone from her past, someone from Munich, and someone that appealed to her. So, I have to assume he was around her age. He's obviously the man she was seen speaking to at Dieter Maier's party. He's obviously who she was having her romantic interlude with, which means he's either the killer, or he likely knows who is."

"And how would you propose we identify him?"

"Well, we're meeting Dieter Maier and his parents in an hour. If they don't know, then I suggest another meeting with the Dettmans. Surely, they would know who he is if their daughter knew him in Munich when they were children."

Vogel sipped his black coffee, just the way everybody in Germany was learning to like it. "And is that it?"

Stadler leaned forward and grabbed his notepad, flipping through it. "I think so. What did I miss?"

Vogel held up the actual diary. "Something you might not have picked up on by holding a copy." He flipped to the last page, dated a week ago, and held it up. "What does this tell you?"

Stadler held up his own last page. "No more than this does."

Vogel snapped it shut, shaking his head in exaggerated disappointment. "You really don't see the significance?"

Stadler stared at the diary. "No, I don't."

"This last entry was dated a week ago."

"Yes. So?"

"That girl wrote in her diary every single day, almost without fail."

"And?"

"And do you think she just suddenly stopped on the last page of her diary?"

Stadler's eyes narrowed. "I have no damn clue what the hell you're talking about. Just tell me and make me feel the fool rather than drag it out."

Vogel chuckled. He tapped the diary. "If she writes in her diary every day, and this one is full, what do you think she did when she wrote that last entry?"

Stadler stared at him and his jaw dropped. "She started a new one."

"Exactly. There's another diary out there, and we have to find it."

Maier Residence

Berlin, Nazi Germany

Stadler whistled as they pulled up to what could only be described as a mansion. The Maiers were prominent Nazis, but they were part of high society long before the Party was even formed in the beerhalls of Munich. They came from old money, and judging from the looks of things, had managed to hold on to most of it, despite the World War and the Great Depression. Stadler stared at his surroundings, mouth agape.

"I can't imagine what it would be like to have money like this."

Vogel agreed. "No point imagining, as police officers, we're never going to know." He eyed his partner. "I thought your family was rich?"

Stadler shook his head. "We're well off compared to most, and only because of my father's position. Nothing compared to this."

Vogel walked up the steps to the main entrance. The door opened before he had a chance to lift the heavy knocker attached to a brass rendition of the family crest. A man he assumed was the butler greeted them. "Kriminalinspektor Vogel, I presume?"

"Yes, and this is my partner, Kriminalassistent Stadler."

The man held the door aside and invited them in. He took their hats and jackets and led them to the drawing room. A few minutes later, after Stadler had made his customary round of the room examining anything and everything, the door opened and the Maiers entered. The father sported an impressive Italian-tailored business suit, his Nazi pin prominently on display. His wife wore a respectable, and no doubt equally expensive dress, and their son was dressed in a jet black, Hugo Boss-manufactured SS uniform. The father, his chest swelled, his chin jutted upward, clearly felt he was above all this. His wife appeared nervous, and their son disinterested.

Vogel held up his ID. "Mr. and Mrs. Maier, I'm Kriminalinspektor Vogel, this is my partner, Kriminalassistent Stadler. Thank you for agreeing to meet with us on such short notice."

"Always happy to help out the Kripo."

"Thank you, sir."

Maier indicated they should sit, and everyone but Stadler did so. Maier eyed him suspiciously though said nothing. "Now, how may we be of assistance?"

Vogel flipped open his pad. "On March fifteenth there was a party at this house."

Maier frowned, aiming a withering look at his son, whose shoulders rolled inward. "Yes, I was made aware of the fact after my wife and I returned from a trip to Obersalzberg. Apparently, it was quite the event. Why, has there been a complaint?"

"No, sir. We're interested in the guestlist for that party."

Maier eyed him. "Why?"

"A young woman named Annie Dettman was in attendance."

Maier's eyes flared. "Not the one who was murdered Friday night?"

Vogel paused, his pen tapping against his chin. "You know of that?"

"Everyone knows of that. When a senior Party member's daughter is murdered, word spreads quite quickly. She was at this party?"

"Yes."

Maier turned to his son. "You know this woman?"

Dieter shook his head. "No, father, there were a lot of people there that I didn't know. As you heard, it got a little out of hand."

"Indeed it did, if my liquor supply is any indication. Do you have any idea how much your social extravagance cost me?"

"I know exactly how much, Father, because you have been telling me over and over for months."

Vogel interrupted. "What about a man, perhaps eighteen to twenty-five, short brown hair, average build, average height, wearing a dark suit?"

Dieter shook his head. "That could have been a hundred people."

"Can you put together a guest list?"

"Only of those I knew, but a lot of people invited others, and then others just heard about the party and arrived uninvited."

"So, if I were to ask you if you knew a young man with a first or a last name that started with the letter A, who was a recent arrival from Munich, you'd have no idea who he was?"

Dieter shrugged. "I'm sorry, sir, like I said, there were so many people here."

Vogel returned his attention to the father. "Do you know Mr. Dettman?"

"Of course I do, though more from a peripheral standpoint. He may be senior in the Party because of his membership number, but the Party is large and quite often people at his level like to think they're more important than they actually are because they've been given a fancy title as a reward for previous service."

"So, Mr. Dettman is not a senior member?"

"Think of how you define a senior officer. General, colonel. Think of him as more of a captain, perhaps a major. Still an officer to be respected, however he could never be thought of as senior. Though like I said, he certainly enjoys giving the impression he is."

"But you have met him?"

"We've been at several of the same functions, and I did have a personal meeting with him several months ago."

"Is the topic something you can discuss?"

"Normally, I wouldn't, however, in light of the fact that Miss Dettman has been murdered, I think it's my obligation to tell you that he arranged a meeting with me to discuss the union of my son Dieter and his daughter, Annie."

Dieter's eyes shot wide. "Are you kidding me?"

Maier held up a hand, silencing his son. "It was a ridiculous notion. Dettman was trying to climb the social ladder through his daughter. I've met his wife, and she's quite an obnoxious woman, the nouveau riche quite often are. I told him in no uncertain terms that I was not interested in his proposal, and that he should be very careful whom he approaches in the future, as it caused great offense, and he might lose the very position he's attempting to secure."

"And how did Mr. Dettman react?"

"He appeared quite embarrassed. He apologized then left. The entire meeting lasted less than five minutes, and we haven't interacted one-on-one since."

"Have you heard of anyone else that he approached?"

"Grumblings."

"Did you ever tell anyone that he approached you?"

"No. Listen, I understood what he was trying to do. Every father wants what's best for his child, and he's trying to find a good match for his daughter. He doesn't deserve to have his reputation ruined over this, however, he shouldn't aim too high as to offend. Irrespective of our common membership in the Party, we are from a different strata of society, and even in normal times, our son would never marry the daughter of a man such as him."

"Would you be willing to put together a list of people he approached, or you think he might have approached? Perhaps one of them wasn't as understanding as you are and took greater offense."

Maier leaned back as if struck. "You don't think..." His voice drifted off. "I can't believe such a thing could have happened, however, if it did, they must be brought to justice. I'll put together a list, on the condition you never reveal it came from me."

Vogel bowed his head. "You have my word, sir."

"Very well."

Maier turned to his son. "And you will write down every single name you can think of who was at that party, and then you're going to call every one of them and find out who they brought. And tell them that's an order from me."

"Yes, Father."

Maier rose and Vogel leaped to his feet. Maier extended a hand, one that hadn't been offered upon their arrival. Vogel shook it. "Please wait here while I put my list together. I'll have my son's list sent to your office by the end of the day."

"Thank you, sir." Vogel handed him his card. "If you think of anything that might be helpful, call me, day or night."

"I will."

The Maiers left the room and the door closed behind them. Stadler turned to him. "Well, that went a hell of a lot better than I was expecting."

Vogel agreed. "Which makes me think we're actually going to get very little useful information here. Let's hope the Dettmans are more helpful."

Dettman Residence

Berlin, Nazi Germany

So far, the case was progressing at a decent pace. What had Vogel concerned was that everyone was cooperating fully. It suggested he wasn't remotely close to finding the killer. If this 'A' person didn't pan out, then they'd be back to square one, and he still had no clue who the third person might be, beyond the fact that it couldn't be 'A' if the descriptions were accurate. And it might still be a red herring.

"Did you find my Annie's killer?" asked Dettman as he and his wife entered the drawing room where they had been shown after their arrival.

Vogel bowed his head. "Not yet, sir, however the case is progressing. A person of interest has come to our attention that you might be able to help us with."

"Of course." Dettman motioned for them to sit. Vogel waited for Johanna to sit as Stadler parked by the window, staring outside.

"Who is this person of interest?"

"We believe he's a friend of your daughter's, though not from Berlin. We believe she knew him from Munich."

They both exchanged glances with each other, glances that were more than just curious surprise. "Oh. Why would you think that?" asked Johanna.

"There was a party six months ago at Dieter Maier's house, and your daughter was there. While at that party, she met a man and spoke to him at length. We found her diary in her locker at work and—"

Johanna Dettman inhaled noticeably.

Vogel paused. "Is there a problem, ma'am?"

She quickly shook her head. "No, no, it was just that I didn't know she kept a diary at work."

Vogel noted the specific words used. "But you were aware she kept a diary?"

Again, she shook her head. "No, no, I wasn't, though I suppose most young girls do."

"The diary we found was full. Its last entry was dated about a week ago, and she seemed to write in it nearly every day, which would suggest there's another diary out there. Is it all right if my partner searches your daughter's room for it while we speak?"

Johanna's eyes widened. "Oh, I don't think that would be—"

Her husband cut her off. "Absolutely. Do whatever needs to be done."

"But those are her private things!"

"She's dead now. If there's a diary in her bedroom that could point to who her killer is, I want it found."

His wife's shoulders slumped. "Yes, I suppose you're right."

Dettman rang the bell and Heidi promptly appeared.

"Show the detective to Annie's room. Answer any questions he might have."

"Yes, sir."

Stadler followed Heidi, closing the door behind him.

"So, I take it there was something in her diary of significance?" asked Dettman.

"Yes, there's reference to the young man she met at the party."

"What's his name?"

"We don't know. She referred to him merely by the letter A."

"A? That could mean anything."

"Yes, sir, it could be an initial for his first name, his last name, or it could merely have been chosen as it is the first letter of the alphabet, though I believe it to represent the young man's first name. Can you think of anyone that she hasn't seen in a long time that would have been a friend from Munich, in her age group, beginning with the letter A?"

They both shook their heads. "Not that I can think of," said Dettman. He turned to his wife. "You?"

"No, but she had so many friends back in Munich."

"Did she have a sweetheart?" asked Vogel.

"Absolutely not!" snapped Johanna.

"Some sort of childhood crush? Remember, this could be back when she was ten or twelve years old."

Again, they both shook their heads. "I'm sorry, I can't think of anybody," said Dettman.

Vogel frowned. "Very well. But if you do think of anyone, please call me. Finding him could be key to solving your daughter's murder."

"Absolutely."

Dettman rose and Vogel followed him out of the room, Johanna remaining behind. He found Stadler coming down the stairs, shaking his head.

Dettman frowned. "Well, that's unfortunate, though if she kept the diary you found at work, wouldn't that suggest that would be where she would keep the new one?"

"We looked, but didn't find it there."

Dettman regarded him for a moment. "When did this diary date back to?"

"She was rather efficient in its use, leaving no blank spaces. She had managed to fit about six months. It appeared to start just before she met 'A' at Maier's party."

"Did the first entry make mention that it was the first time she had written?"

Vogel shook his head. "No, which has me thinking there are older volumes."

Dettman frowned. "It makes me wonder where all the others are. I'll have the staff search the house top to bottom. Those diaries have to be somewhere. We have quite a few boxes stored from our old home, perhaps they're in there."

"Perhaps."

Vogel and Stadler left the house and climbed into their car. As they pulled off the property, Stadler, his knee jumping the entire time, spun toward him. "I may not have found a diary, but there was definitely one kept there."

"Explain."

"I found a rather fancy pen in her nightstand drawer with a conveniently empty spot where a diary much like what we found would fit."

"And what makes you think that it wasn't simply where the one we found was stored until she moved it to her place of work?"

"Because the pen had dripped and the ink was still wet."

"A leaky pen isn't exactly much of a clue."

"Perhaps." He held up an empty ink bottle. "But I found this in her trash bin. I asked how often they were emptied, and Heidi said every day while the family eats lunch, though they were ordered not to touch her room yesterday. Doesn't this suggest she refilled her pen after lunch Friday?"

Vogel's head bobbed slowly. "Yes, though it could have been to write a letter."

Stadler stared at him. "You're just not going to give me this one, are you?"

Vogel chuckled. "No, I'm just doing what any good detective should do. Question the evidence. I'm not dismissing it, I'm just challenging it like it should be challenged."

"So, what are you saying?"

"I'm saying that she wrote something very recently. Since she was at work the last time the bin was emptied, she must have refilled the pen when she came home from work, before she left for her rendezvous."

Stadler scratched his knee. "So, what we're saying is she came home and wrote an entry in her diary just before she was to have a romantic interlude."

Vogel nodded. "That would suggest this particular entry might be quite revealing. And if someone found and removed the diary between then and when you went into the room, it suggests that whatever was written in it was indeed something they didn't want us to find."

"Us, or anyone?"

Vogel pursed his lips. "You're right. Anyone."

"Who do you think would do such a thing?"

"It could be anyone in that household, though I find it highly unlikely that a staff member would do it."

"Well, perhaps if they were aware of the diary, and they found out she was murdered, one of them might have taken it to protect her dignity." Stadler frowned. "What about the parents?"

"Mr. Dettman certainly appeared not to be aware of it, however, I thought Mrs. Dettman was a little too eager to deny knowledge of its existence."

"A mother would know, wouldn't she?"

"A mother might, and a mother who was so concerned about her daughter's future, might actually read it while her daughter was at work."

"So then she might have read the final entry."

Vogel nodded. "Yes, she very well might have. The question is, did she read it before her daughter was murdered or after?"

Stadler's eyes shot wide. "Oh, my God, her hair is the same color as the one we found! Do you think the third person could be the mother?"

Vogel tilted his head slightly, grimacing as his partner finally caught up to the notion tormenting him since yesterday. "It's a definite possibility, but why would she kill her daughter? She'd be more likely to kill the man she was with. If her daughter's dead, then there's nothing she can do for the family's future. And why kill anyone? Just grab the daughter and take her out of there."

"What if we got a sample of her hair? Could Naumann compare it to the one that was found?"

"How do you propose we get that sample?"

Stadler frowned. "Yeah, I suppose there's no way."

"No, before we start letting the Dettman family know that Johanna is a suspect, we need a lot more evidence than we currently have."

"So then, what do we do now?"

"Well, we should have the guestlist for the party by the end of the day. We'll have the Orpo run them down. We already have the list of potential suitors for Miss Annie, though I'm not sure we want to go rattling those cages just yet."

Stadler agreed. "You have to give Mr. Dettman credit. He certainly had grand ambitions for his daughter, based on those names."

Vogel agreed. The short list of names provided by Dieter Maier's father, only half a dozen, were ones he recognized, all senior members within the Nazi Party, all wealthy. "I don't think he took in to account the fact those families would want their own sons to marry well, and a working-class Nazi is so far below them on the social ladder, they would barely notice him."

"Perhaps that's why Mr. Maier became aware of these people being asked. They thought it was a joke."

"It's definitely possible." Vogel glanced at his watch. "We still have to interview her rival at the shoe factory. Teufel said he'd arranged for her to be there by two. Let's grab a bite to eat and then we'll head over."

Stadler rubbed his stomach. "Sounds good to me, I'm starving. Your place again?"

Vogel chuckled at the hopeful tone. "Don't get too attached to my wife's cooking. Not today. She gabs with her friends after church, especially if I'm not there. Let's just grab something near headquarters."

Stadler appeared disappointed.

Vogel glanced at him. "You really do like my wife's cooking, don't you?"

Stadler smiled at him. "I wasn't lying when I said that was the best thing I had eaten in years."

"Then I'll make sure I invite you over more often."

"I'd appreciate that, sir."

Vogel guided them toward headquarters, shocked at how quickly things had turned between him and his partner, and despite the gruesomeness of the case they were working on, he found himself enjoying the work more than he had in some time. He didn't trust him yet, nor did he think he ever would completely, but at least the young man wasn't the total asshole he had thought. There was a human beneath the tough Nazi shield that he could perhaps, in time, be true partners with, for he needed someone to talk to about the job, someone he could trust without worrying they would go running to some Nazi, betraying his innermost thoughts.

For there were some things you just couldn't talk about with your wife.

Dettman Residence

Berlin, Nazi Germany

Dettman watched through the window as the detectives left the property. The moment they were out of sight, he headed back to the drawing room where his wife still sat. He closed both sets of doors, securing them, then sat beside her. "You know who they're talking about, don't you?"

She stared at him, her eyes flaring, then she quickly turned away. "No. No, I don't."

"Yes, you do, and so do I."

She lifted her head, her mouth agape. "You do?"

"Yes. You and I both know that they're looking for Arland."

"How can you be sure?"

"Those two were inseparable when they were children."

"But they were just children. There was nothing romantic there."

"No, but they were best friends, and now that they understand such things, is it so hard to believe they might pursue those feelings?"

His wife sighed. "No, I suppose not. If only we had known in time, we could have put a stop to it." Her shoulders sagged. "I might have been able to save her."

He eyed her for a moment. They hadn't spoken much of the loss, both tip-toeing around the subject, the wound far too raw to risk tearing afresh. The moment he would mention anything, she would withdraw and leave the room, her sobs filling the household from the confines of their bedroom. Eventually, they would need to talk about it. He was hurting too, and his wife was the only person he could speak with freely, without worrying some report would be filed with the High Command.

His thoughts turned to the young Arland who had been such a good friend to their daughter when she was growing up. He was about the only thing that Annie was truly upset about when they moved here six years ago. She had always been a bit of an introvert, despite his wife's assertions she had many friends. When she had been very young, she had been painfully shy, and they had to literally pry her off her mother's leg just to get her to school on that first day. But she had slowly opened up, and a big part of that was because of Arland.

Arland was shy as well, though not as much as their daughter, and had helped drag her out of her shell, albeit slowly, and when the two were together, they were like any other two children, laughing, smiling, running around, doing what children should be doing, and if they had stayed in Munich, he had little doubt they would have become each other's first love, and perhaps even been married by now, a child conceivably on the way.

And it was that possible future that had him thinking there was no way Arland could kill Annie. Yet it had been six years, Arland had been but a boy, and people changed.

The police said she had lost her virginity during this encounter, and that it appeared voluntary, at least that's what the inference was. If that were the case, then whatever change Arland had gone through had obviously not been noticed by his daughter, because he couldn't imagine her lying with anyone whom she didn't completely trust. And it was that belief the boy couldn't possibly be guilty of this crime, that had him lying to the police. But if Arland were involved, if he had indeed murdered their daughter, then he must be brought to justice, and if he were innocent of the crime, he might just know who was guilty of it.

He stared at the clock sitting on the mantel, a wedding gift from his parents that had cost them far more than they could afford. His position had allowed him to improve their lives dramatically, as well as those of his siblings. And as he sat there, he thought of all the lives that depended upon him. It wasn't just his wife and daughter. It was his parents, his wife's parents, his brother and sister, her brother. There were just too many people reliant upon him. If it were to come out that he had lied to the police, and as a result, protected his own daughter's killer from justice, it would destroy his reputation, and they could lose everything.

Yet he couldn't bring himself to believe that Arland was the murderer.

A thought occurred to him and he rose, startling his wife.

"What is it, dear?"

"I have to make a phone call, then go into the office."

"It's Sunday, and our daughter has just been murdered. Why would you possibly go?"

"It has nothing to do with work, and everything to do with our daughter and our future."

Wilhelmine Ring Residential District

Berlin, Nazi Germany

Arland shivered, still unable to warm up after having spent the night outside. He was cold and hungry, a vicious mix when combined with his state of mind. He needed a safe place to pull himself together, but he could think of nowhere to go. He had no real friends in the city, most men his age in the Army, and of those, most were stationed outside of the area. Those who weren't, didn't hide their contempt for people like him whom they felt were making excuses for not joining the fight.

It had kept him lonely since arriving in Berlin, and he found himself recessing into the shell he once occupied as a boy. The first time he had gone out since arriving was when a young woman from his office had invited him to Dieter Maier's party. He had been delighted to go, borrowing his father's only good suit to try and fit in, but had found it a gathering of souls to whom he simply couldn't relate.

Then he had bumped into Annie.

Annie!

His shoulders shook. He still couldn't believe she was dead and that he was responsible. He had no idea what he should do. He could turn himself in and confess to everything he knew, yet how could that possibly bring justice for everyone? He needed time to think, some safe place to go where he could collect his thoughts. He sighed. If he did think about it, the only people he knew in the city that he could trust were Annie's parents.

Yet to see them now, after what had happened, was unthinkable.

He leaned forward, hanging his head between his knees as the tears flowed. His squeezed eyes couldn't rid themselves of the image of Annie, her throat slit, her body littered with stab wounds. He could open his eyes and remove the image, yet he deserved to suffer with the memory, he deserved to suffer until they looped the noose around his neck and hanged him until he was dead.

"You all right, boy?"

His heart leaped into his throat as he jerked upright, wiping the tears from his eyes as he stared up at a uniformed police officer. "What?"

"I said, 'Are you all right?'"

"Yes."

"Did you sleep here last night?"

He shook his head, knowing the truth might get him in trouble. "No, I just felt like going for a walk before the day started."

"What's wrong? What's got you in such a state?"

He wanted to tell the man everything, to confess to all he had done, all he knew, to get it off his chest, yet this wasn't the time or place. He decided to tell a partial truth. "I lost my girlfriend."

The man's head tilted back. "Ah, young love. It burns so intensely while you're in it, and even more so when you're out. We've all been through it, son, and you'll go through it again, most likely. But I can tell you from experience, you'll get over it and you'll find a new love, and in time, you'll forget this one that's broken your heart."

"I suppose so." Yet the words rung hollow, for there would never be anyone else in his life. Annie had been his soulmate, the chances of them reuniting after so many years apart incalculable. And now that she was dead, slaughtered after a blissful evening together, the first for both of them, he was certain she would be the last love he would ever know, for even if he did manage to survive, he could never bring himself to look upon another woman without seeing her face, the shock on it, the fear, the betrayal.

I can't go on like this. I deserve to die.

"Go to church, son. Confess your sins. Then ask one of the pretty young things there out for a walk. Perhaps you just might find the next love of your life." The officer patted him on the shoulder. "You have a good day now." He strolled away.

Arland opened his mouth to confess everything, then stopped himself. "You too, sir."

He rose, straightened himself as best he could, then headed for the nearest church, its spires just ahead, not to seek a future love, but to confess his sins and seek the advice he so desperately needed.

Reich Chancellery

Wilhelmstraße, Berlin, Nazi Germany

Dettman sat behind his desk at the newly constructed Reich Chancellery, the old one described by the Führer as suitable for a soap factory but not the new Reich. Construction had been completed in two days shy of a year, with over 4000 men toiling day and night to meet the Führer's ambitious timeline. They had succeeded, though only if one ignored the glaringly obvious—none of the fittings had been installed. Now, the building was substantially complete, and working here was an honor and a pleasure.

It was a little quieter than usual since it was Sunday, but was still busy. After all, war didn't take a day off to rest. His office's job was to vet patronage appointments. If a Party member wanted to reward someone for their loyalty or a job well done, or merely to get them off their backs, it was his office that would do the background check.

It was rare that he would deny a request, but it was rarer still that he would approve one. His job was to merely flag any problems so that the person making the request could then decide whether they wanted to move forward with it. Someone higher than him would make the ultimate decision, so if the appointee would end up being an embarrassment later down the road due to something Dettman's office missed, he had no doubt he would take the blame. That was why he prided himself on doing a thorough job for each and every request. It had given him the skill set and the tools to vet the young men he had been considering as his future son-in-law.

Though that was all done with now.

His chest tightened, and he was about to lose control yet again, when there was a knock at the door. He drew a deep breath, centering himself before answering. "Enter."

His aide, Corporal Friedel, stepped inside, holding up a file. "I have it, sir."

The file was handed over and Dettman flipped through it, cursing to himself when what he feared was confirmed. Arland and his family had been transferred to Berlin six months ago. He had hoped to find that Arland was still safely in Munich, ruling him out as a suspect. But with him in Berlin, there had to be little doubt now that he was either the killer of his sweet Annie or, at a minimum, was involved.

"Thank you for this. Dismissed."

His aide hesitated. "Sir, there's something I have to tell you, though it would betray a confidence."

Dettman stared at him. "This confidence you speak of, would you be betraying your country?"

"No, sir."

"Your Party?"

"No, sir."

"Your uniform?"

"Absolutely not."

"Then out with it."

"Yes, sir, of course, sir. The file that you have, I didn't just…I didn't get it from Central Records today."

"What do you mean?"

"I mean, I already had it."

"What?" Dettman stared at him. "What do you mean you already had it?"

"Someone requested the file a week ago."

He gripped the arms of his chair, his heart pounding. Whoever had requested that file had to be involved in the murder, or perhaps was the murderer himself. There was no way this was a coincidence. "Who requested the file?"

Friedel shifted uncomfortably.

"Out with it."

"Sir, it was your wife."

Engel Gasthaus

Berlin, Nazi Germany

Vogel wiped his mouth and tossed the cloth napkin on his empty plate. He leaned back and stretched as Stadler hurried to finish his own lunch, his young partner having flapped his gums for most of the meal. It was clear he now felt much more comfortable with his senior partner, and was finally asking all the questions that should have been asked a year ago, personally and professionally.

Vogel was more than willing to answer most of them, and when something was asked that could lead them into uncomfortable territory, he would guide his protege in another direction. Politics and the war, and the effects of both, were topics that should never be discussed with a partner from such a devout Nazi family.

Fritz, a former Kripo detective, now proprietor to a gasthaus across the street from headquarters, walked over. "How was everything, gentlemen?"

"Fantastic, as usual."

"Ha! We're subject to the same rations you are, so I know you're lying."

Vogel laughed. "Yes, I know, and for you to be able to make what I just ate taste so good with such limitations, is a testament to how great a chef you are."

Fritz slapped him on the back. "You know me, I can't cook for shit, but I'll pass on the compliment to my wife, though I think the real secret is that she's sleeping with the butcher so she gets a better cut of meat than everyone else around here." Stadler's eyes shot up and Fritz laughed, slapping the young man on the back. "Don't worry, it was my idea."

Vogel roared with laughter, Fritz tossing his head back and joining in, Stadler uncertain as to whether he was being had.

Vogel pulled out his wallet and Fritz waved a hand. "Your money's no good here."

Vogel frowned. "Well, I was all right with that before the war, but everybody's hurting now. You'll take my money and you'll be happy about it."

Fritz eyed him and tilted his head toward Stadler. "How about I just charge him double?"

Vogel grinned. "Sounds good to me."

Stadler stared at them, still confused. He reached for his wallet and Vogel let the fun continue. Stadler pulled out enough bills to cover both meals and placed them on the table.

Fritz chuckled, jamming a thumb at the young man while looking at Vogel. "You've got a keeper here."

"I think I might."

Vogel placed his own bills on the table then regarded his partner. "One thing you're going to have to learn in this business, is that almost everything that comes out of an ex-cop's mouth is either a joke or a lie, and that I pay for all my own meals."

Stadler blushed, returning the excess money to his wallet. "I don't know what the hell just happened, but when the war is over, the two of you should get a comedy act together. I think you'd be a hit."

Vogel regarded his old friend. "Wolfgang and Fritz?"

Fritz scrunched up his nose. "Nah, I don't like the sound of that."

"Fritz and Wolf?"

Stadler waved a hand. "Forget your names. How about the Kripo Geezers?"

Vogel and Fritz glared at him, and he shrunk in his chair. They both laughed.

Vogel drained his beer. "By the time I retire, that just might be the perfect name for the two of us." He rose, shaking Fritz's hand. "Good to see you, my friend. Next time I'm working on a Sunday, you'll see me here."

"We're open other days, you know?"

Vogel grunted. "We're not all successful businessmen like you who can afford to eat all their meals out."

"I know, I know, and I appreciate every pfennig you give me. When this is all over, you and I are going to get together and get drunk like the good old days."

Vogel patted the man on the arm. "I look forward to it. It's the next day that I'll regret."

"All pleasure comes with an equal amount of pain."

Vogel said his goodbyes then he and Stadler walked across the street to headquarters.

"I can't believe I've never eaten there before."

"You've never deserved to be invited."

Stadler eyed him. "And now I deserve an invite?"

"Yes."

"Why?"

"Because, since yesterday, you haven't been a complete asshole."

Stadler chuckled as he held open the door. "Any other secret gasthauses you're keeping from me?"

"Plenty, but let's see if this new you isn't just a fad first."

"Detective! Had a good lunch?"

Vogel patted his stomach at Sergeant Abel's question. "Excellent. Fritz's wife was really on her game today."

"She does make a mean schnitzel. I think I'll be going over on my break." He pointed toward their offices. "An envelope was dropped off for you a few minutes ago."

"Who dropped it off?"

"It was an aide to Mr. Maier."

"Thanks." They headed into the office and Vogel sat at his desk, Stadler sitting across from him, frowning.

"That was sooner than expected."

Vogel agreed. "Yes, it was. It makes me wonder just how complete a list we're being provided with."

He opened the envelope sitting on his desk, pulling out a sheaf of papers with a sloppily written list of names that had attended the party, suggesting Dieter Maier had written it personally. It was several pages long with a note at the bottom.

I'll send more should I discover any additional names.

Vogel shook his head, holding up the pages. "This is a half-assed attempt at best. There's no way he had time to call these people and flesh out this list."

Stadler folded his arms. "What do you think that means?"

"It could mean the Maier family feels this is beneath them, though for Mr. Maier to provide his list, suggests he's taking it seriously. I get the impression Dieter Maier isn't, or Dieter Maier knows something and is trying to hide that fact."

"Which do you think it is?"

Vogel leaned back, scratching his chin. "I don't know, but the Maier family isn't one to annoy unless it's absolutely necessary." He handed the list over to Stadler. "Give this to the sergeant. I want all the names run down and uniformed officers interviewing them to find out who was at the party, and to see if anyone remembers our suspect speaking to Annie." He checked his watch and rose. "Let's get to the factory and speak with Annie's rival."

Stadler followed him. "Do you think she's the one who belongs to the stray hair?"

"If I did, I wouldn't have waited to arrange a meeting at her place of employment the next day. I would've been on her doorstep immediately after I found out about her. I think this is simply going to be petty jealousy, but we can't rule anything out because of that hair. It could simply be nothing at all, or the key to everything."

Approaching Vogel Residence

Berlin, Nazi Germany

Sofia always felt good after church, though with her husband busy working an apparently high-profile murder case, he hadn't been able to attend with them. It wasn't an infrequent occurrence, and it always disappointed her, for she enjoyed going as a family. She was proud of her husband and what he did, and the members of their congregation were fully aware why he wasn't on the front during a time of war.

Crime still occurred, people were still murdered, and someone had to bring them to justice.

And in Germany, it meant trained men, men who had years of experience working with the criminal mind and bringing those who would commit evil to justice. Many in the congregation were good friends, the rest acquaintances she was always happy to see. In these stressful times, the support of one's church always helped her forget, if only for a few hours, the troubles that surrounded them.

Church had been well-attended this morning, as it usually was. With the Allies bombing the city, everyone wanted to make sure they were in the Lord's good graces should a stray bomb take out their home rather than a factory. Their neighborhood hadn't been hit yet, thankfully, though how long they would remain lucky, she wasn't sure. There were more stories exchanged after church and at tea of someone knowing someone else who had lost someone in a bombing. And the fourth and fifth-hand stories were now becoming second and third.

It was a terrible thing, this war, and she couldn't understand why the Führer had got them into this mess. The country had been doing so well. People were working, people were happy again, people were fed, the streets were clean, the damage suffered after the World War and the Great Depression almost wiped away.

And now their cities were being bombed and food was rationed once again.

She helped the children off the tram then strolled happily toward their apartment, humming a tune she couldn't get out of her head. She loved music, but their gramophone had broken months ago, and getting it repaired was an unnecessary luxury. Perhaps one day they might afford to get it fixed, though she would never dream of asking her husband something so selfish.

She looked both ways, then crossed the street. She was a little behind schedule, lingering after church longer than usual, something she often did when her husband wasn't able to attend because of his job.

"Mommy, I need to go to the bathroom."

She glanced at her daughter. "We're almost home, dear. Can you hold it?"

"I don't think so."

"Well, try, honey."

She picked up the pace and the three of them scurried the final block to the apartment. She pushed the door open for the stairwell and the kids rushed through. She was about to follow them when a hand appeared in front of her face, clasping over her nose and mouth. A knife flashed before her eyes then the blade pressed against her neck.

A mouth was at her ear, a man's hot breath causing her to cringe. "I have a message for your husband. Back! Off!"

Her entire body trembled and tears flowed as the stairwell door closed shut.

"Do you understand me?"

She nodded rapidly.

The door opened and it was her son, Daniel. His jaw dropped and his eyes shot wide at the sight. She was suddenly let go and she couldn't bring herself to turn to see if the man were indeed gone, but his footfalls and then the opening and closing of the rear door to the apartment building suggested they were now safe.

Daniel rushed forward, wrapping his little arms around her legs, his shoulders heaving, and as the stairwell door shut once again, she caught a glimpse of her little girl standing on the first step, trembling wide-eyed as urine flowed down her leg, pooling on the floor at her feet.

Dettman Residence

Berlin, Nazi Germany

Dettman entered his house, his mind a fog of confusion as he blindly handed over his hat and jacket, barely registering his actions. "Where's Mrs. Dettman?"

"I believe she's in your bedroom, sir."

He headed up the stairs, taking each step slowly, the revelation that his wife had requested the file on Arland consuming him. He had challenged Friedel on why he had put through a request from his wife, and the young corporal had said she wanted to find out more about him as a potential suitor for their daughter. There was no way his aide could have known this was a lie, for no one knew the history between the two families that had once been so close in Munich.

He opened the door to the bedroom and stepped inside, finding his wife at her make-up table. She turned and smiled at him. "You're home!"

His expression must have revealed his mood, for her face clouded over. "What's wrong?"

"Why don't *you* tell *me*?"

Her cheeks paled. "What do you mean?"

"Don't play innocent with me. Friedel told me everything."

Her shoulders slumped. "Then you know."

"Did you really think you could keep this secret from me?"

"No, I suppose not."

"Why? Why did you request the file? And you did it a week ago! What possible reason could you have had?"

She opened one of the drawers in her table and pulled out a small book. "I found this."

He eyed it. "What's that?"

"It's our daughter's diary."

His eyes widened. "Did the servants find it in their search?"

She shook her head. "No. And they wouldn't."

"What do you mean?"

"I burned them all."

His jaw dropped. "You did what?"

"I had to protect her. When I found this one last week…" She closed her eyes. "It's so personal. I searched her room and found the others. When I found out what happened to her yesterday, I burned them. I couldn't stand the thought of the police reading our daughter's most personal thoughts."

"Then why did you keep this one?"

"Because I wanted you to read it. You need to know what our daughter was up to."

"I don't want to read it."

"If you knew what it contained, you'd want to."

He sat on the settee at the end of the bed, filled with trepidation, for he wasn't certain he wanted to know the answer to the question he was about to ask. "What does it say?"

"This is her newest diary. It started only a week ago, and from what she wrote, it's quite clear that she and Arland had been in a secret relationship for many months now."

His chest deflated. "So, it was him that she was seen with at the party. He is this 'A' that they referred to."

"Yes. She made a reference to their childhood in Munich. I knew it had to be him, but I couldn't be sure. That's why I went to Friedel and asked him to run his name to find out if he was in Berlin. Once I knew, then there was no doubt she was betraying us, she was betraying her family and its future security. Something had to be done."

His heart raced as his fists clenched. "Please tell me you're not responsible for our daughter's death."

Her head dropped, her shoulders shook, and her tears flowed. "I'm so sorry."

Reich Chancellery

Wilhelmstraße, Berlin, Nazi Germany

Corporal Friedel sat fidgeting at his desk, unsure of what to do. His boss' daughter had been murdered, and as far as he was aware, the murderer was still at large and as yet unidentified. But the coincidence of Johanna Dettman and her husband asking him to pull the same file on the same young man was simply too much, and the fact she had lied about her reasons convinced him even more that something was going on here. The young man was from Munich and had only recently arrived in Berlin. The Dettmans were originally from Munich as well. He didn't dare pull their file to see if there were any intersections in their history, but again, the coincidence was just too much. They obviously had their suspicions about him, though her request predated the murder by a week. Surely, if she thought her daughter was in danger, Johanna would have taken action.

But she hadn't, and her daughter was now dead.

Dettman's orders had been to tell no one, and he was compelled to obey him. However, Dettman wasn't military, and surely justice should take precedence. He couldn't believe that Dettman wouldn't want his daughter's murderer brought to justice, and the only reason he had come up with for the order, was that Dettman was protecting his wife. What she had done was a crime, but technically nobody knew, as he had put the request for the original file through under Dettman's name. No paper trail could possibly lead back to Johanna. Only he and the Dettmans were aware she had made the request. He had little doubt that once Dettman was thinking clearly, the man would realize his wife wasn't in any danger.

From what he knew about criminal investigations, time was of the essence, and if Arland was the murderer, the police had to know sooner rather than later. This was simply too important not to be shared with the police. He stared at the phone, debating what to do, then sighed, closing his eyes for a moment.

He pulled out the card that Vogel had given him during their first encounter and tapped it on the desk several times, the internal battle between duty and justice raging.

Vogel Residence

Berlin, Nazi Germany

Sofia sat in her chair, rocking rapidly as her trembling hands attempted to deliver the calming tea she so desperately needed. She had cleaned up her daughter and given them both snacks, putting on as brave a face as possible. They were both in their room now, hopefully napping as she had instructed them, and prayed they would soon forget the sight of their mother with a knife pressed to her throat by a strange man.

She stared at the phone, a luxury few had, installed by the police department when her husband had become a detective. She had to tell him what had happened. Of that, there was no doubt. But when should she do it? She could call now and perhaps reach him, though it wasn't a message that could be left with the Desk Sergeant. The man had said to tell her husband to back off, but back off what? She assumed it had to be a case he was working on, and if he were to heed the warning, no one at the office could know.

She sighed. She had to do it in person. She checked the clock on the mantle. Dinner was still hours away, and there was never any guarantee he'd be home for it. The very idea, however, of him not knowing what had happened and not getting the message had her fearing for his safety. What if he needed to back off now? If he didn't find out for hours, something could happen to him before he returned home.

But she knew her husband. He would never back off, he would never let himself be threatened. Yet the fact the warning had been delivered meant whoever he was investigating was aware of this fact, and that knowledge might cause him to be more cautious. She shuddered at the thought that whoever it was knew where they lived. How was that even possible? The home addresses of police officers weren't exactly publicized.

Last night, when the children had been put to bed, he had given her a few details on what he was working on, about the poor girl murdered and how she was the daughter of a senior Party official. Those were the type of people who could find out where a detective lived, and they were exactly the type of people who would deliver a warning they would expect heeded, and if it weren't, wouldn't hesitate to kill her entire family to protect whatever it was they were hiding.

A knock at the door had her yelping, her cup of tea, barely touched, spilling some of its contents onto the saucer. She placed the dishes carefully on the table, the glass clinking with every shake of her hand.

There was another knock.

She stared at the door, struggling to remember if she had locked it, and though she was certain she had, she couldn't convince her panicked mind that it was telling her the truth.

"Sofia, it's me, Ingrid."

Her shoulders slumped and she sighed in relief. She pushed to her feet and hurried to the door as Ingrid knocked again. She unlocked the door and opened it. Ingrid's smile immediately faded, replaced by concern.

"Oh, dear, what's wrong?"

Sofia stepped back, letting her friend inside, then closed the door, rapidly locking it behind them.

"What's happened?"

She shook her head. "Nothing I can talk about."

Ingrid was one of her best friends. She had known her for years, which was why she was fully aware the woman had no filter—she was a chatterbox, anything said to her would be repeated to untold numbers over the coming days. But she also knew her friend would never be satisfied until she gave her an answer.

"Something's wrong. Tell me, maybe I can help."

Sofia shook her head, returning to the living room and taking her seat. "It's nothing. I just had a little fright."

"What? What happened?" asked Ingrid as she sat across from her.

"Nothing. We just…Christina almost got hit by a car. I'm still a little shaken."

"Oh my! Is she all right?"

"Yes, she got scared, had a little accident. Everybody's just a little shook up, but we're all fine. Hopefully, she'll forget it soon enough. Don't mention it to anyone. She's embarrassed enough as it is."

"I understand."

Sofia eyed her friend. "Why are you here?"

Ingrid frowned. "I'm afraid I did something rather foolish that I hope won't cause you any problems, but I felt duty-bound to tell you."

And as her friend told her what had happened yesterday, a rage formed in the pit of her stomach and she shot to her feet. "Can you watch the children?"

Ingrid's eyes widened. "I suppose. Why?"

"Because I have to see my husband immediately."

Adi Dassler Shoe Factory

Berlin, Nazi Germany

Vogel sat across from Frieda Brack, Stadler occupying his usual position in the corner behind her. She was dressed as well as any young woman could be expected on a Sunday, and her demeanor suggested she considered herself far above anyone with whom she was sharing the room. The file they had pulled on her indicated her family was wealthy and well connected within the Nazi Party. Her supervisor Teufel suggested she had been forced to work here by her parents to show the family was contributing to the war effort, and she was not pleased with that fact.

"How well did you know Annie?" asked Vogel.

She shrugged. "Not very well."

"Did you ever socialize with her outside of work?"

"Never."

"And why is that?"

"She's fake."

His eyebrows rose slightly. "What do you mean?"

"I mean just that. She's fake. There's no way anyone who doesn't have to work here is so happy about it."

"Just because you don't like it, doesn't mean nobody should. From all accounts, she got along well with her coworkers, all except you."

"They're all fake. How anybody could be happy working here is beyond me."

"Were you the only one who didn't get along with her?"

She shrugged again. "I try to pay as little mind as I can to these people."

"I'm told you went out of your way to try and make her life miserable."

She tossed her head back, laughing. "If I really wanted to make her life miserable, she would've killed herself rather than gotten herself killed."

Vogel regarded her. "That's rather cruel to say, considering she's dead."

"What do I care? This is war. We're all going to die anyway."

"Not a very patriotic attitude to think the Reich is going to fail."

She laughed. "I know my history. Things were going well in the World War at the beginning, then look what happened. Once the Americans get involved, we don't have a chance."

Vogel eyed his partner, bristling in the corner. "In your apparently limited dealings with Annie, were you aware of any young men who may have been paying her extra attention?"

Her cheeks flushed. "Everyone was sneaking stares at her. She was such a tramp. She invited it."

"How so?"

"I don't know. She was nice to everybody. She should have discouraged any flirtation, especially from people like this. They're beneath her, but then from what I heard, they really aren't. Her father was a paper pusher in Munich before they moved to Berlin. He didn't deserve his position. He just happened to be a drunk at the same beerhall where the Party was founded."

"For someone who doesn't care about her, you seem to know a lot about her family."

Her jaw squared, but she said nothing.

"So, now that we've established you *do* take a great amount of interest in her, is there anyone in particular that paid her more attention than usual?"

She folded her arms and leaned back. "No, not that I can think of."

"Were you aware she was meeting someone Friday?"

"No." She perked up. "Was she meeting with a boy?" She huffed. "Scandalous. I knew she was a tramp."

"Where were you Friday night?"

She stared at him. "Do I look like a boy to you?"

"Just answer the question."

"My father was hosting an event at the house. I was there with dozens of witnesses. Just because I didn't like her doesn't make me a murderer. Don't try to get me mixed up in this. If you damage my family's reputation, you'll regret it."

Vogel handed her his card. "If you think of anything that might be helpful, let me know, day or night. And remember this, while you might not have liked her, she was the daughter of a senior Nazi official. If you bring us information that leads to the arrest of her murderer, it would only enhance the reputation of your family." He rose. "You can go home now."

She left the room, saying nothing, and he closed the door behind her. Stadler pushed off the wall.

"She's a piece of work, isn't she?"

Vogel agreed. "Definitely a bundle of hate there."

"I pity whoever she ends up with."

Vogel chuckled. "Me too. Unfortunately, that was a dead end as expected. Let's head back to the office. Hopefully, our guys canvassing that list will have had better luck."

Kriminalpolizei Headquarters

Prinz-Albrecht Straße, Berlin, Nazi Germany

Sergeant Abel glanced up from the report he was reading, his eyes widening at the sight of Sofia Vogel rushing in, clutching her purse against her chest. "Mrs. Vogel, what are you doing here?"

She flinched and squinted at him. That was when he noticed her entire body was trembling. The poor woman was terrified. He stepped around his desk, approaching her.

"Has something happened?"

She nodded, though said nothing. He stepped back to search for any signs of injury or a struggle, but she didn't appear disheveled, and there were no signs of injury. And then he saw it. A distinct thin line on her neck. In his decades of experience, he knew exactly what that was.

Someone had held a knife against her.

"Come with me. Your husband's not here right now, but I'll find him for you."

She still said nothing as he led her to an interrogation room where she could be alone and preserve her dignity and that of her husband.

"I'll be back in a moment. You just wait here. If you need anything, you know where to find me." She sat down, still clutching her purse. He closed the door and headed for the captain's office. He rapped on the door, rattling the glass, and was waved in.

"Yes, Sergeant?"

"Mrs. Vogel just arrived. I believe she's been assaulted. There's evidence a knife might have been pressed against her neck."

"And what does she say?"

"Nothing. The poor woman is terrified."

"Where is she now?"

"I put her in Interrogation Room A so she could have some privacy."

"Good, good. Do we know where her husband is?"

"He's at the Adi Dassler Shoe Factory, interviewing a witness. I expect he'll check in shortly."

"Put a call out on the radio. Find out who's closest and get someone to that factory. He'll want to be back here as quickly as possible."

"Yes, sir." Abel closed the office door and headed to the front desk. He called dispatch then grabbed a glass of water and a shot of schnapps, bringing them into the interrogation room. He placed both in front of Sofia, pushing the shot glass a little closer. "Drink this, it will calm your nerves."

She shot it without hesitation, grimacing at the bitter taste.

"Do you want me to get you another?"

She shook her head.

"I put out word for your husband to come back as soon as possible. Hopefully, he'll be here shortly."

"Thank you."

They were the first words that had come out of her mouth, and he took the opportunity. He knelt beside her, a terrifying thought having occurred to him. He had seen it on so many occasions, a woman raped, and in her embarrassment and shame, cleaning up to make herself presentable.

"Is there anything I can do for you? Get you a doctor? A…umm…nurse?"

Her eyes darted up and she stared at him for a brief moment, horror in her eyes, then shook her head rapidly. "No, no, it's nothing like that!"

He exhaled loudly in relief. "Thank God for that." He patted her hand. "I'll be at the front desk. Your husband will be here as quick as can be."

She clutched her purse tighter, but said nothing. He left the room, closing the door, and said a silent prayer of thanks that whatever had happened to her wasn't what he had feared. But someone had pressed a knife against the woman's neck, someone had terrified her, and it was something serious enough, she felt compelled to share it with her husband immediately. It suggested to him a sense of urgency surrounded whatever had happened.

He sat behind his desk and picked up the phone to see if dispatch had heard anything, not envying what Vogel was about to go through, likely imagining the worst when he received word of his wife's need.

Adi Dassler Shoe Factory

Berlin, Nazi Germany

Vogel stepped out the front door of the factory, followed by Stadler, their interview with Frieda Brack bearing no fruit as he had expected. This was the thing about police work. Most of it was tedious, monotonous, and completely uneventful. The crime movies before the war were often laughable. He had seen some from America before the restrictions, and if they were anywhere near the truth, he felt sorry for those people. That amount of gunfire and death was unfathomable here. Crime was lower now that the war had begun. With most crimes committed by men, especially young men, that was to be expected. Remove millions of men from their homes and send them to fight wars in foreign countries, then of course crime would be reduced. Yet during times of war, other types of crimes became more prevalent.

Desperate people did desperate things.

That included petty theft and an explosion of the black market. And the black market meant you had to have suppliers. Those suppliers could be at the street level, those same petty thieves he despised so much, corrupt bureaucrats pilfering supplies intended for the citizens of the nation, or enterprising border officials who facilitated the movement of illegal goods across various borders, including Switzerland and Spain.

One's local grocer might be a primary contact, but there was no way he would be the brains behind the operation—he simply wouldn't have the connections. Someone else would be providing him with the supplies, and there could be many hands involved through the entire supply chain.

And the higher up the chain, the more brutal and vicious they became.

Selling someone a little bit of extra butter than they're entitled to, might seem a harmless crime. But that butter had to come from somewhere, and it wasn't from some farmer with a little excess supply. It was ultimately from someone who had stolen that butter, butter no longer available for your neighbors or the soldiers on the front.

It was why he would have no part in it, despite the fact his wife's friends, and most people he knew, took part. He used to get mad at her when she would bring things home after visiting her friends, but he gave up, especially when he saw how happy it made their children. Part of him still wanted to tell her to refuse, yet it was hard enough for the family of a police officer to have friends. These days, too many people were afraid the spouses of police officers, especially now that they had been transferred under the command of the SS, would report back anything untoward they had seen to their husbands.

Fortunately, Sofia had several good friends she had known for years, and that had met him on many occasions. They were well aware he wasn't that type of man, and well aware he investigated homicides, not the black market. That was an entirely different department.

Tires squealed to his left and they both spun toward the sound. A vehicle surged toward them then screeched to a halt, a uniformed officer poking his head out the window. "Kriminalinspektor Vogel, I have an urgent message!"

Vogel's eyes widened slightly, and he exchanged a look with his partner. Something must be truly urgent for a message to be delivered in such a manner, and it could mean only one thing—there was a break in the case.

"It's your wife, sir! Something has happened!"

His strength rapidly flowed out of his body. He gripped the roof of the car to steady himself and took a breath but said nothing.

Stadler stepped forward. "What's happened to Mrs. Vogel?" The concern in the young man's voice was genuine and heartfelt. And appreciated.

"I don't know, sir. I just have instructions to get you the message that she's at headquarters and you need to return immediately."

"Let dispatch know we received the message and are on our way."

"Yes, sir."

Stadler stepped around the car as the other unit left. "Sir, let me drive."

Vogel handed his partner the keys. Stadler gripped him by the shoulder, giving him a gentle shake.

"Sir, she's all right. If she were dead, she wouldn't be at headquarters, nor would she be there if she were injured. Something's happened, but she's all right."

Vogel inhaled deeply then blew the breath out before nodding. "Yes. Yes, of course. Let's get to headquarters." He climbed into the passenger seat as Stadler fired up the engine, heading toward headquarters.

Vogel closed his eyes in an attempt to calm himself, yet was forced to open them as all he could picture was his wife, bloodied and bruised. Or worse. He had worked enough cases over the years to know there were plenty of ways a woman could be viciously assaulted with no evidence left behind that would be detected by a cursory examination. He thought of young Annie and how, at first. they thought she had been raped, and it had him wondering if whatever had happened to his wife was connected to the case.

If it were, it could mean only one thing.

They were getting close.

Wilhelmine Ring Residential District

Berlin, Nazi Germany

Arland sat quietly in the church, staring at the cross in front of him. It was Sunday, and the service had been packed. He couldn't remember the last time he had attended. It was undoubtedly before his sister had died. They had all lost faith that day, and he had lost his best friend days later when Annie's family suddenly moved from Munich without warning.

Gabriele had been so innocent and so young. He had just turned 13, and she was only six. How she had gotten out of the house, he didn't know. She had been found drowned, tangled in the reeds down by the river. The theory was that she had tried to feed the ducks and had fallen in. He had been out with his parents, where, he couldn't remember, his young mind having blocked much of the memories of that day. All he could remember was returning home to the news that his sister was dead.

And the wails of his mother.

The last memory he had of that day was sneaking a peek inside his sister's bedroom where the adults were gathered, the reeds still wrapped around her wrists and ankles. He just thanked God he hadn't seen her final moment frozen on her sweet innocent face.

"You've been here for hours, son. Is something troubling you?"

He flinched at the voice, the priest having approached unnoticed in his reverie. He shook his head. "No, Father, I'm all right. I just needed somewhere to collect my thoughts."

The old man patted him on the shoulder. "Stay as long as you want, my son. And should there be something you wish to discuss, I'll be in the rectory or the confessional, should you so desire."

"Thank you, Father." The priest shuffled away and Arland turned his gaze to the cross, still uncertain as to what to do. He wanted justice, not only for Friday night, but for what had happened to his sister, so long ago, and he still had no idea how to achieve it.

Kriminalpolizei Headquarters

Prinz-Albrecht Straße, Berlin, Nazi Germany

Vogel shoved the doors out of his way as he stormed into headquarters. Sergeant Abel pointed to his right.

"She's in Interrogation Room A, sir."

Vogel said nothing, instead, heading swiftly toward his wife. He stepped in front of the door and forced himself to calm down. Whatever had happened, the last thing she needed was to be confronted by his fear and concern. Calmed, he gently turned the knob and pushed the door aside. His wife was sitting at the table, clutching her purse to her chest as if it were a pillow that might provide some comfort. She looked up and her eyes widened. She leaped from her chair and rushed into his arms, sobbing uncontrollably. And with each shake of her shoulders, his worst imaginings turned into reality, for something genuinely horrible must have occurred.

He wrapped his arms around her protectively, then lowered his chin and kissed the top of her head, letting her vent her emotions without saying anything, instead gently rubbing her back. He did this not only for her benefit, but for his own, as any words spoken at this moment by himself would be fractured, for he too was torn apart at the thought of what had happened to her.

When he finally felt he could control his voice, he gave her an extra squeeze before relaxing his grip on her slightly. "Why don't you tell me what's happened?"

She sniffed and he retrieved a handkerchief from his pocket. She took it and wiped her eyes, then blew her nose. That was when he noticed the mark on her neck and a pit of rage formed inside as the concern for what his wife had experienced progressed into an unquenchable desire for revenge. He tilted her head back and smiled.

"You're safe now. Just tell me what happened, no matter what."

She stared up at him, her eyes red, the tears still flowing. She shook her head slightly. "It isn't what you're thinking."

"You weren't…"

She shook her head. "No, I wasn't."

His shoulders sagged as he exhaled. He kissed her on the cheek. "Thank God for that. But something has you upset, and you're the strongest woman I know. So whatever it is, must still be bad." He guided her to the chair then pulled another beside her and sat, taking her hands. "Tell me everything."

And as she told him about the events of earlier, of the man pressing the knife against her neck saying he had a message for her husband, "Back off," the pit of rage consumed him. And when his wife, gasping for breath, described what had happened to his little girl, he snapped to his feet and paced.

"I'm going to find him and I'm going to kill him. Nobody scares my family."

"There's more."

He froze and turned toward her. "More?"

"Ingrid showed up at the apartment shortly after, and she told me that she had said something to the grocer, Luft. She was afraid he might have got the wrong idea that you were investigating the black market."

Vogel tossed his head back and growled in rage. "That woman is insufferable! I can't believe you're still friends with her! She never knows when to keep her mouth shut!"

"Don't be mad at her. That's just the way she is. You know that. And she did come and tell me what she had done. She didn't have to do that."

He clenched his fists. "And that's the only reason I'm not telling her husband what she did." He drew a breath and held it for a moment. "Can you describe the man?"

She shook her head. "I never saw him. But…" She stopped.

"But what?"

"But Daniel might have seen him."

Vogel closed his eyes for a moment, exhaling loudly at the thought he might have to question his son, and perhaps even his daughter.

And then a thought occurred to him. "Where are the children?"

"They're at home with Ingrid."

He was about to scold her for leaving them with the woman who might have caused this, but bit his tongue. Ingrid wasn't the guilty party.

She was a fool, yet he trusted her with his children. The woman had no filter and was only happy if her gums were flapping, whether with food, drink, or talk. He was convinced this had nothing to do with the murder. The timing was too coincidental, and those who might be involved in the murder would know that delivering a message as simple as "Back off" would be meaningless. The case would merely be handed off to someone else, as it was too important to ignore.

But a black market investigation involving a grocer where his wife and her friend shopped? That was personal, that was close to home. And if they thought his wife was involved in the investigation, which was an idiotic notion, they very well might think a personal warning could have the desired effect.

Though they were wrong on all accounts.

Now, he not only had a murderer to catch, but he had a black marketeer to deliver a message to as well.

Dettman Residence

Berlin, Nazi Germany

Dettman gripped the photo of his daughter, clutching it to his chest as his world fell apart around him. His daughter was dead, and his wife was responsible. The moment she had apologized, he had left the room. He couldn't take to hear the words she was about to say. No explanation could justify what she had done.

Her obsession with this lifestyle had changed her. She was no longer the woman he had married. She had once been such a loving soul, drawing contentment from taking care of her family. But now, all she cared about was being perceived as an equal to those with whom they were now associated. What she failed to understand, was that they never would be accepted. He had been a clerk, working day in and day out pushing paper, and she had tended to the family and cleaned the houses of those with far more money than they could ever dream of having.

It had been a good, simple, honest life, but a hard one, which was why he went to the beerhall far too often. And by mere luck, that beerhall was where the future Führer and the others gathered on a regular basis to spread the word of their cause.

If he hadn't been the type to drink away his problems, or if the fledging Nazi Party had simply chosen a different place to meet, he wouldn't be where he was today. A tear rolled down his cheek unnoticed. If any one of those things hadn't have occurred, they would still be living in Munich, he would still be pushing paper, his wife would still be cleaning homes, and Annie would still be alive.

He stared at her picture, the tears flowing freely now, as he realized it was an oversimplification. His assumptions were based upon their lives six years ago, before he had called in a favor to save his family's reputation. They had buried what had happened all those years ago, no one ever mentioning it, protecting Annie by hiding the truth. And should that truth now come out, it could destroy what remained of the family, and they would lose everything.

He sighed. The family was already destroyed. His daughter was dead, and his wife had done something unforgivable, all to maintain a way of life they never should have embraced.

But she was his wife and he loved her, and she was all he had left. He had to protect her no matter what she had done. And at the moment, there was only one person who was aware she had become involved. He closed his eyes, then picked up the phone, connecting to a number he thought he never would. In his position, he collected a lot of favors. He never took a bribe, despite many being offered. But on countless occasions, a satisfactory outcome was achieved, with the other party shaking his hand and stating something along the lines of, "I owe you one."

And today, he was about to collect on a debt.

"Hello?"

"This is Dettman. I need somebody taken care of."

Kriminalpolizei Headquarters

Prinz-Albrecht Straße, Berlin, Nazi Germany

Stadler stood in the hallway outside the interrogation room, curious as to what was going on. Abel had told him nothing, and he understood the desk sergeant's reasons. There was no trust there. Nobody in this building trusted him, and it was his fault. Over the past couple of days, his relationship with his partner had improved significantly. Merely by opening up and telling him the truth about his situation, had resulted in the first ever invitation to dine with his partner's family. He had been truly touched, and hoped it would be the first of many.

He saw how the other detectives interacted. They were on such good terms, such close friends. They trusted each other implicitly, and he wanted the same. The age gap between the two of them was significant, yet that didn't seem to be a problem with the others.

The softening of Vogel's feelings toward him, and the fact he had just dined with the man's wife yesterday, had his heart aching with genuine concern. And though he projected cold-heartedness as a defense mechanism, that wasn't him. Yes, he was a Nazi, and proud of it. He would die for his country. He would die for the Reich. He would die for his Führer.

But that didn't mean he had to be heartless.

His father was a true senior Nazi. Not like Dettman. Stadler had grown up in the Hitler Youth, indoctrinated from a young age into the cause, and none of that bothered him. His life was one of privilege, though he had vague recollections of things being much different before the Nazis gained power. Everyone's life was more difficult back then, what with the Great Depression in full swing, even more so in Germany than the rest of the world due to the punishing reparations forced upon them by the Treaty of Versailles. He blamed the apologist Weimar Republic, founded at the end of the war, displacing the monarchy that had led them into the conflict.

Yet that was the past.

Now that he lived on his own, no longer bombarded continuously by his father's vitriol and that of his brothers, he found himself tolerating those who held different beliefs than him a little more each day. Yes, his partner and all of his coworkers were members of the Nazi Party, but it wasn't by choice. Some of them fully embraced the ideals like he did, but many others didn't. At first, he had a problem with that, though eventually he came to understand that these were still honorable men who had taken the oath so they could continue their essential jobs.

Crime as it had once been was mostly wiped out, replaced with other forms. And as he knew all too well, murderers still murdered, and he wondered if whatever had happened to Sofia was related to their case.

After all, senior Nazis were involved, and they would stop at nothing to keep their secrets.

The door opened and he stood straight. Vogel stepped out first. "Give me the keys. I'm going to take my wife home now."

He handed them over. "Is she all right?"

"She will be. I'm going to take her home and then come back. I'll tell you everything then."

"Yes, sir. If you want, why don't you stay with her and I'll go through the reports, and we can get a fresh start in the morning?"

Vogel shook his head. "No, we need to deal with something right away." A piece of paper was pressed into his hand. "Find out where he lives."

Stadler glanced at the name, not recognizing it. "Yes, sir. I'll have it for when you get back."

"Good."

Vogel pushed the door open again and his wife emerged. She forced a smile and Stadler snapped his heels together, bowing, immediately regretting his instinctual gesture of respect as the poor woman flinched.

"I'm sorry, ma'am," he murmured. "I hope you're feeling better soon."

She said nothing as Vogel led her down the hallway. Stadler kept a respectful distance, then walked ahead to hold the door open for them. He pointed to the right. "It's parked right over there, sir."

"Thank you."

He watched them make their way to the car, then he closed the door, heading for his desk. He sat down and grabbed the phone, unfolding the piece of paper, wondering why it was that Vogel wanted him to locate Manfred Luft, owner of Luft Family Grocery.

Reich Chancellery

Wilhelmstraße, Berlin, Nazi Germany

Friedel sat at his desk, staring at the file for Arland Nicklas, a file requested not only by his boss, but his boss' wife. He still had no idea why they were so interested in the young man, though he suspected it had something to do with their daughter's murder. The fact Johanna had requested the file a week ago, suggested that if this Arland person were indeed connected, then the Dettmans were possibly involved in the killing of their daughter, and that was unforgivable. Yet he couldn't quite bring himself to believe that was what had happened. What was more likely, was that Arland was the murderer, and Johanna had her suspicions about him. She had requested his file to protect her daughter, but still hadn't saved her.

Whatever the case might be, the police had to be made aware, for though he was a loyal Nazi, he also had his principles, and hiding the identity of the potential murderer of your own daughter was reprehensible. The truth had to come out, and the only way it could, would be for him to reveal it.

Yet the call he had placed to Vogel remained unreturned.

A door creaked then footfalls echoed through the empty hallway beyond his office door. Nobody should be here on a Sunday at this hour, not in this section of the building. His heart rate picked up and he eyed the drawer containing his sidearm.

His phone rang, startling him. He grabbed it and pressed it to his ear. "Mr. Dettman's office, Corporal Friedel speaking."

"Corporal, this is Kriminalassistent Stadler, returning your call."

He breathed a sigh of relief. "I need to meet with you and your partner about something of the utmost delicacy. There's something you need to see."

The footfalls stopped.

"Does it relate to the murder of Annie Dettman?"

"Yes."

"Is Mr. Dettman aware that you're contacting us?"

"No, and it's best he doesn't."

"I see. Can this wait until tomorrow?"

"No."

"Very well. Why don't you come to headquarters?"

"No, I can't be seen there. It's best if you come here. That way, if we're seen together, people will believe you came to see me under your own volition, rather than me requesting the meeting."

"Kriminalinspektor Vogel isn't available right now, but I can come over, if that's sufficient."

The footfalls receded.

"Yes, sir, that would be fine."

"I'll be there in fifteen minutes."

"Thank you."

He hung up the phone, listening for the footfalls, but they had stopped yet again. He grabbed the file off his desk and slipped it into an envelope. He quickly addressed it to Vogel then scribbled a note, stuffing it inside. He sealed the envelope then stuck it in the middle of the pile of outgoing messages.

His heart slammed as he heard something at the door. The doorknob turned and he gulped. He pulled open his desk drawer, reaching for his sidearm when the door opened, a Luger leading the way.

Vogel Residence

Berlin, Nazi Germany

Vogel sat on the edge of their bed, his wife lying in it, propped up against the headboard, having calmed dramatically since they had left headquarters. While she had bathed, he had spoken to Daniel and confirmed that the boy had seen the man who had threatened his mother, though only for a brief moment, and was unable to provide any useful details.

"Why did he do that, Daddy?"

"Do you remember the play last year at your school?"

Daniel nodded.

"And how people acted, how people pretended they were scared or happy or sad?"

"Yes."

"Well, that's what you saw. Your mommy and her friend were acting."

"She seemed really scared."

"That's because your mommy's an excellent actress."

"So, it wasn't real?"

He forced a laugh. "Of course not. You and your sister are always safe with me or your mommy. So, you believed she was scared?"

"Yes."

"Do you think she should be in the play?"

His head bobbed furiously. "Yes!"

"I'll tell her you said that. When your sister wakes up, let her know that it was all just a game."

"I will, Daddy."

He grunted at the memory, his wife raising a questioning eyebrow. "I can't believe our son bought my story."

She chuckled. "He's ten. He still doesn't know that his father lies to him from time to time."

"Good thing." He patted her hand. "Ingrid has agreed to stay until I get back."

Her face clouded. "Do you think they'll come back for me?"

"Absolutely not. It was a warning delivered to me, and I'm pretty sure I know who delivered it. If they were to harm the family of a police officer, every single cop in this city would come down on them so hard, they'd be finished. They know that."

"What are you going to do?"

"Don't worry about that. I'm just going to take care of the problem so that we never have to worry about them again."

"You're not going to do something stupid, are you?"

He grinned. "Who, me?"

She wagged a finger at him. "Don't go making things worse."

He became serious. "Don't worry. I've dealt with these people for years. I know how to speak their language."

"Well, don't go alone. Bring Otto with you."

"Don't worry, he's waiting for me at headquarters."

He leaned over and kissed her on the forehead. "You get some rest. If you need anything, have Ingrid take care of it. She owes you big time after what she did."

"So, you think it was because of her, and not the murder you're working on?"

"Yes. The people I'm dealing with would never have bothered with a warning."

She shuddered. "Sometimes, I wish you weren't a police officer." She reached out and wrapped her arms around his neck, holding him tight. "Be careful."

He returned the squeeze. "I always am." He let her go and left the room. Ingrid leaped to her feet.

"Is she all right?"

"She will be."

"I'm so sorry for what I said."

He jabbed a finger at her, staring at her sternly. "You need to get control of that mouth of yours. The next person you betray might not be so lucky."

Her face paled and she fainted.

He caught her, directing her into her chair, then headed out the door, not giving a damn about the irresponsible woman that had put his family at risk.

And having no doubt she hadn't learned her lesson at all.

Reich Chancellery

Wilhelmstraße, Berlin, Nazi Germany

"Pardon me," said Stadler as he stepped aside to let a man charging through the doors pass. The man said nothing, instead hurrying down the steps then striding briskly across the courtyard. The light was fading now, and he couldn't make out any details about the man, beyond that he was tall and slender and wore a long, dark leather jacket, something favored by the SS and Gestapo.

Stadler stepped inside and presented his credentials.

"Who are you here to see?"

"That's confidential."

The corporal frowned. "I'm not sure I can let you in."

"You do realize I'm Kriminalpolizei? That means I'm a member of the SS."

"Yes, sir. However, this building belongs to the administration, and therefore I answer to the Party, as do you."

Stadler frowned. "Very well. I'm here to see Corporal Friedel from Mr. Dettman's office."

"Do you have an appointment?"

"I do."

The man picked up the phone, dialing the extension. It rang several times and then he shook his head. "I'm sorry, sir, but there's no answer."

Stadler eyed him. "That's odd. I spoke to him less than fifteen minutes ago. He's expecting me." He turned toward the doors. "Who was that man that just left?"

"Sir?"

"The man that just flew past me when I came in here. Who was that?"

The corporal shifted in his seat. "I'm sorry, sir, but I can't say."

"Can't or won't?"

The man stared at his clasped hands. "Is there a difference, sir?"

Stadler grunted. "No, I suppose not." He turned on his heel and headed for Dettman's office.

"Sir, you can't go up there!"

"Try to stop me."

He rushed up the stairs two at a time as he drew his sidearm. He sprinted down the hallway, Dettman's office at the far end. The door was closed, but a sliver of light was visible underneath. He turned the knob and shoved the door aside, then gasped in horror at the sight of Corporal Friedel, slumped in his chair, a hole in his head.

Kriminalpolizei Headquarters

Prinz-Albrecht Straße, Berlin, Nazi Germany

Vogel entered headquarters, finding it fairly quiet in the evening hour. It wasn't like in the old days where people would swarm the place with their petty grievances. As soon as that SS symbol had been added to the front of the building, their foot traffic had reduced dramatically. No one ever wanted to interact with the SS unless it was absolutely necessary.

Abel hailed him from his front desk and Vogel checked the time.

"Didn't your shift end hours ago?"

"It did, but Elias asked if I could cover for him. His brother was injured in the bombings last night, so he's helping get him settled until his parents arrive from Düsseldorf."

"Is he going to be all right?"

"Apparently, yes. But his days of working the factory floor are probably over with."

Vogel winced. Elias was a good man in the twilight of his career, and he assumed his brother was of a similar age. And if he were injured bad enough that he could no longer work, he had just become a burden to his family. And the state.

Abel beckoned him and leaned across the desk, lowering his voice. "How is your wife, sir?"

"Shaken, but she'll be fine."

He could tell Abel desperately wanted to know what had happened, and rather than have speculation run rampant throughout the building, as he had no doubt it already was, he gave him a partial truth. "She was accosted on the way home after church. A mugger pressed a knife against her throat, demanding all her money. The children witnessed it and they were all quite upset."

"That's terrible! Any chance you'll be able to ID the perpetrator?"

"No. She didn't see his face. He came at her from behind, and the children were too scared to notice any details. I'm afraid this one's going to go unsolved unless we hear of other reports in the area and get lucky."

"I'll put the word out. Sometimes luck is on our side."

Vogel flashed a smile. "Do that."

The phone rang on Abel's desk. "Pardon me, sir." He picked it up as Vogel headed for his office.

"Sir!"

Vogel turned.

"I have Stadler on the line for you."

Vogel's eyes narrowed. "He's not here?"

"No, sir. He left about half an hour ago. He didn't say where he was going."

"Put it through to my desk."

"Yes, sir."

Vogel hurried to his desk, wondering where his young partner had gone off to after they had agreed to meet here to take care of his wife's situation. He picked up the phone and pressed the button for the extension. "Otto? Where are you?"

"Sir, I am at Dettman's Office. Corporal Friedel has been murdered."

"What? He's been murdered? How?"

"Single shot to the head."

"When did this happen?"

"Just minutes ago. I might have actually seen the murderer leaving the building."

"You were already there?"

"Yes, sir. It's best we discuss this in person."

He frowned, but didn't press. It was apparent his partner didn't want to say anything more over the phone. "All right, I'm on my way."

He slammed the phone down on the desk, and headed for his car. Abel flagged him down, waving a file. "Sir, this just arrived for Stadler. Do you want it, or should I put it on his desk?"

He was about to tell him to do just that when he paused. "What is it?"

"An urgent request he made for anything on Manfred Luft."

Vogel grabbed the file. "I'll give it to him." He headed out the door, debating what was more important. Dealing with Luft now, or heading to the murder scene. His duty was clear, but a dead man would be just as dead an hour from now. He flipped open the file and found Luft's home address, mentally locating it. It was sort of on the way.

His decision was made.

Luft Residence

Berlin, Nazi Germany

Vogel grabbed a baton from the trunk of the car then entered the apartment building and climbed the two flights of stairs to Manfred Luft's unit. He double-checked to make sure the hallway was empty, then knocked on the man's door. Footsteps approached on the other side, then the latch clicked. He prepared himself, the baton gripped in his right hand, behind his back and out of sight, as he had no way of knowing who was about to answer.

The door opened and Luft's eyes widened in surprise. "Mr. Vogel!"

Vogel reached forward, grabbing him by his shirt and yanking him into the hallway. He shoved him against the wall and slapped a hand over his mouth as he pulled the door closed. He pressed the baton against Luft's neck and pushed hard, cutting off his flow of oxygen. "You know why I'm here."

The terror in the man's eyes betrayed that the son of a bitch knew exactly why. He nodded.

"You crossed a line. Tell me who you gave my wife's name to."

He eased up on Luft's neck and the man gasped for breath. "I'm so sorry, Mr. Vogel! I didn't want anyone to get hurt!"

Vogel shoved the baton harder once again. "I don't want excuses or explanations. I want names." He eased off.

"It was Drake, Drake Pankow."

Vogel had never heard of the man. "How do I reach him?"

"I have a number for him."

"Do you have an address?"

"No, but he'll be making a delivery to the store tomorrow morning at six."

Vogel backed away, but pressed the tip of the baton against Manfred's throat. "I'll be there tomorrow morning at five-thirty. If you give him any warning, I'm coming back, and I promise you *will* live to regret what I do to you."

Vogel headed for the stairwell, and as he pushed through the door, he glanced over his shoulder to see Luft still standing there, his back pressed against the wall, shaking in terror. He wanted to lay a beating on the man, to punish him for the part he had played, but he had known him for years. Luft was a good man, for the most part. So many were involved in the black market, that if they were to arrest everyone, there'd be no stores left to serve the public, and few public left to shop regardless.

The black market was thriving and was too well-accepted in a country that had sent so many of its young men off to fight a war few privately wanted. Beating Luft within an inch of his life would accomplish nothing beyond self-gratification, and if word got out that he was the one who had delivered the beating, it would be his family that would be shunned. Luft had merely made the phone call. He hadn't sent the man that had terrorized his family. There were only two people who truly merited the pounding he had planned for them, and that was the man who had held the knife, and the man who had sent him.

Reich Chancellery

Wilhelmstraße, Berlin, Nazi Germany

Security was tight at the massive complex housing Dettman's office and much of the Reich's administration. Vogel flashed his ID and was directed toward a staging area. Police, Army, SS, and Gestapo were everywhere. This wasn't an ordinary murder. This was an assassination of a soldier of the Reich in a government building that should have been secure.

He finally gained access to the building and headed up the stairs then down the long corridor toward Dettman's office. It was jammed with personnel, few, if any, that needed to be there. He muttered a curse under his breath as he stepped into the office and found at least ten people there, only two of whom he recognized—his partner and Medical Examiner Naumann. He shook his head.

"Anyone who doesn't need to be in here, get out now!"

The entire room turned toward him, a Wehrmacht major bristling. "And just who the hell are you?"

"Major Ostwald, that's Kriminalinspektor Vogel. He's in charge of the investigation," replied Stadler.

"You're contaminating my crime scene. I want everybody out of here now."

Ostwald glared at him then tilted his head toward the door, everyone heading out. Vogel forced himself to calm down. He stepped in front of the major, lowering his voice. "Sir, you, of course, are welcome to stay."

This placated the man. "I'll assist in any way I can, Kriminalinspektor."

"Thank you." Vogel stepped over to the body. "So, Naumann, did we interrupt your evening?"

Naumann glanced over his shoulder at him, revealing a bow tie. "I was at the opera with my wife."

"Sorry about that."

"No need to apologize. I hate the damned opera. In fact, next time I'm going, I'm telling you, so you can have me hauled out of there again."

Vogel chuckled. "Consider it done." He gestured toward the corporal. "Looks fairly straightforward."

"Yes, it does. It looks like—"

Vogel cut him off and turned to Stadler. "You've been here the longest. Why don't you run down the crime scene for us?"

Stadler smiled slightly, recognizing he was being tested. "Yes, sir." He pointed at the door. "The door was closed when I arrived, and only the desk lamp was on."

Vogel stepped over to the wall and turned off the lights, restoring the scene to how it had been discovered. "Like this?"

"Yes. The corporal was slumped forward on the desk, single gunshot wound to the head, no powder burns. I suspect he was shot from the doorway."

Vogel glanced at Naumann who concurred. "Continue."

Stadler stepped toward the desk and indicated a drawer. "This was opened as it is now. I took a look inside. There's a sidearm."

"And what were you doing here?" asked Ostwald.

The slight flaring of Stadler's eyes told Vogel that this was a piece of information that had to be kept to themselves.

Vogel snapped a finger up, glancing over his shoulder at Ostwald. "I'll be asking the questions, sir. But if you must know, I had sent my partner here to ask the corporal some follow-up questions into our murder investigation."

"And what could the corporal possibly know?"

"As I'm sure you're aware, Major, I cannot reveal any details of an ongoing investigation. However, rest assured, they were relevant. They concerned the murder of Mr. Dettman's daughter. I'm sure you wouldn't want to compromise that investigation."

Ostwald paled slightly. "Of course not."

Vogel examined the desk for anything obvious. He glanced at Stadler. "Didn't you say you thought you passed the killer?"

"Yes, sir."

Vogel turned to Ostwald. "I assume there's a sign-in log."

"Absolutely. This building is secure."

Vogel jerked his chin toward the corpse that contradicted this assertion. "I think he might disagree."

Ostwald frowned. "Yes, I suppose."

"Major, if you could be so kind as to go to the front desk and bring us the log. We need to know who came into this building this evening."

Stadler cleared his throat. "And you might want to question the corporal who was manning the desk. I think he knows something."

"At once," said Ostwald, who promptly headed out the door, leaving just the three of them in the room.

Vogel turned to Stadler. "All right, what's going on?"

"The corporal called me, said he had to meet you. He had something important related to the case that we needed to see. I asked him to come to headquarters, but he refused. He said he couldn't be seen there, and that he wanted us to come to him so that he could claim he had nothing to do with the meeting."

"Did he say what information he had?"

"No, he wouldn't discuss it over the phone, though he did confirm it had to do with the case."

Vogel stared at the desk. "Well, if he had something to give us, it's not here now. The killer must have taken it." He stared at their victim, then back at the door. He turned back toward the desk, his eyes coming to rest on the half-open drawer that contained the man's sidearm. "If I'm the killer, I'm not going to open that door slowly. I'm going to open it, come in, and shoot. Yet the corporal had enough time to open the drawer before he was shot. Does that seem plausible?"

"I don't see why not," said Naumann. "Door opens, man walks in with a gun, the corporal reaches for his, and is shot before he has a chance to get his hand on it."

"Yes, but remember, the door opens, our killer is going to have his weapon out already, and aimed in the general direction of where his target is going to be. Friedel would have a split second to react. Remember, just because a door opens, doesn't mean a killer is walking through. You're going to assume it's something innocent, then you only have a split second to react when you recognize there's a gun in play. For him to have had the time to reach for the drawer and pull it open halfway before he was shot? I just don't see it happening."

"What are you suggesting?" asked Stadler.

"I'm suggesting he either knew, or suspected, that whoever was coming through the door meant to do him harm, so he was already reaching for the gun." Vogel held up a finger and cocked an ear, the sounds of footsteps and chatter in the hallway quite evident in the silence of the room. "That hall would've been empty at this time of night. If anyone were coming, he would've heard their footsteps."

Naumann's eyes narrowed. "But if he was suspicious and he heard them coming, why wouldn't he have already had his weapon out, ready to defend himself?"

"Because he was doing something else!" exclaimed Stadler. "He was hiding whatever it was he wanted to give us."

Vogel gestured at the desk. "Everything seems in order here. I see nothing that suggests this was searched."

Naumann nodded. "I agree."

"So, if he was hiding what he wanted us to see, then unless the killer knew exactly where to look, it must still be in here." He pointed at the corporal. "Search him, see if he's got any papers on him." Naumann began a search and Vogel leafed through the pile of outgoing messages as Stadler started trying filing cabinets, finding them all locked. About halfway down the pile, Vogel stopped at an envelope.

An envelope with his name on it.

He pulled it out. "I think I've found it."

There was a rap at the door and it opened without waiting for permission. Vogel's back was still to the door. He folded the envelope in half, then half again, before stuffing it inside his jacket. He glanced over his shoulder. It was the major and a terrified young corporal. Ostwald held up the logbook.

"According to this, only six people logged in during the hour preceding the arrival of your partner, and none in the half hour preceding it."

Vogel turned to the corporal. "Who was the man my partner saw leaving?"

The corporal's eyes darted to the floor. "I don't know who you're talking about, sir."

Stadler stepped forward. "That's impossible. There's no way he didn't see him leaving the building. He's lying."

Vogel closed the gap between him and the young corporal. "If you continue to lie to us, then I'm going to charge you with interfering in our investigation, an investigation into the murder of not only Corporal Friedel here, but of the daughter of a senior Nazi Party official. Now, while I might not have you tortured and killed, do you think they'll hesitate?"

"I...I can't tell you what you want to know."

"Why not?"

"Because they *will* torture and kill me and my family."

"Who's they?"

"I can't say."

"But there is a 'they.'"

The corporal nodded.

Ostwald turned to the young man, keeping his voice gentle. "Son, we'll protect you."

The corporal rapidly shook his head. "No, sir. Even you can't protect me."

Vogel stepped a little closer, lowering his voice. "Gestapo?"

The man's eyes shot wide and the color drained from his face. He said nothing, but he gave Vogel one single nod of his head.

Everyone in the room tensed. Vogel regarded the young man for a moment before making a decision. "Let the record show that the corporal cooperated fully. He never saw anyone suspicious enter the building. It's our opinion the murderer gained entry using some other manner than the front entrance, or had already been hiding inside the building. He saw the murderer leave, but only saw him from behind and was unable to provide a description other than he was of average height and average build. Before he had a chance to report the incident, the murder was discovered, and once given the opportunity, he reported what had happened to his commanding officer. The record will show that the Kriminalpolizei are satisfied he knows nothing that can help them in their investigation. Are we all agreed on that?"

Stadler, Naumann, and Ostwald all nodded.

"Good. Then you're dismissed, Corporal. I recommend you return to your post and finish your shift. I'll make sure it's known that we gained nothing useful from you. That should protect you."

"Yes, sir. Thank you, sir."

Ostwald opened the door. "It's unfortunate you didn't see anything useful, Corporal," he said in a slightly raised voice for the benefit of those in the hallway.

The corporal frowned, still shaking. "Yes, sir. I'll try to be more vigilant next time."

"You do that."

The corporal headed down the hallway, all eyes no doubt on him as Ostwald closed the door. He lowered his voice. "If the Gestapo did this, they didn't do it without orders."

Vogel had to agree. "Major, your continued cooperation isn't necessary. I'll understand completely if you want to excuse yourself."

Ostwald stared at him for a moment and it was apparent an internal debate was raging. He drew a breath then exhaled loudly, shaking his head. "One of my men has been murdered while on duty. Bringing the perpetrator to justice is my responsibility, no matter what the risk to me."

Vogel had to admire the man. Most people would have jumped at the opportunity to remove themselves from the path of the Gestapo. They were brutal, as ruthless as the SS were, but their duties intersected the public far more than the SS did. If you were an enemy combatant and were captured by an SS unit, your worst nightmares would likely come true. And if you were a Jew or member of the extensive list of undesirables named by the Nazi Party, you would be shown no quarter.

But the Gestapo went beyond that. The citizenry of the Reich were too often subjected to their tactics, yet no one acted without orders. Ostwald was correct in that. If the Gestapo were indeed behind this murder, the assassin had been given orders to do so.

Vogel pointed at the door. "Secure that."

Ostwald stepped over and pressed his shoe against the bottom of the door frame. Vogel fished the envelope out of his jacket pocket and unfolded it, then tore it open. He pulled out the pages inside.

"What is it?" asked Stadler.

"It's a file on the Nicklas family, including a nineteen-year-old son named Arland."

Stadler's eyes shot wide. "A!"

"It could be." Vogel took another look in the envelope and spotted a small piece of paper at the bottom. He retrieved it. "Now this is interesting."

"What?" asked Naumann.

"It says, 'JD requested this file one week before the murder. HD requested it the day after the murder and wasn't aware JD had done so already.'"

"JD and HD?" asked Ostwald.

"Johanna and Hermann Dettman."

"And just who is this Arland Nicklas?"

"If he is who we think he is, he's the secret boyfriend of our victim."

"You think he's the murderer?"

"He's our most likely suspect, yes. We know she was meeting him the night she was murdered." Vogel pointed at the phone and handed the file to Stadler. "Call headquarters. Have four men meet us at this address immediately."

"Yes, sir." Stadler picked up the phone, placing the call.

Vogel turned to Naumann. "Can you handle things here on your own?"

"Absolutely. Go catch that piece of shit."

"Good. I'll send a couple of my guys up just in case crowd control becomes a problem."

Ostwald cleared his throat. "Don't worry about that. My men will be able to keep that mob outside under control."

"Very well." Vogel turned to Naumann. "If I were you, I'd get this body back to the morgue as quickly as possible before somebody comes in and tries to claim it."

"The truck is outside. All I need is a stretcher, a body bag, and two strong men."

"I'll send two of my men up with what you need," said Vogel.

Stadler handed the pages back, the phone call complete. Vogel stuffed the file into his inner pocket again and patted it. "Nobody mentions this. Agreed?"

Everyone did.

Vogel headed out the door, the chatter in the hallway ceasing, those gathered staring at him as if he might be about to give them a briefing they could go home and gossip about to their wives. Instead, he marched briskly toward the stairs and then out of the building. He flagged down two uniformed *Orpo, Ordnungspolizei,* officers, then pointed at the Medical Examiner's truck. "Get a stretcher and body bag then bring them up to

Medical Examiner Naumann. He's with the body. Help him bring it out, then escort him to the morgue. Don't let anyone interfere."

"Yes, sir." They both rushed toward the truck as Vogel and Stadler headed for his car. Stadler tossed a set of keys to another officer and pointed at a vehicle nearby.

"Return that to headquarters when you get a chance."

"Yes, sir," smiled the young officer, getting to drive a rare treat for many of the more junior members of the force.

Once they were secure inside the vehicle and off the grounds, Stadler couldn't keep his excitement bottled up anymore. "Who do you think ordered that assassination?"

Vogel fished the file out of his pocket and handed it to Stadler. "You tell me. Does that look like a family that has connections to the Gestapo powerful enough to order the murder of a Wehrmacht soldier on government property?"

Stadler pulled out a flashlight and clicked it on. He quickly read through the file. "They're from Munich, arrived six months ago."

"Yup. Quite the coincidence, isn't it?"

"The timing certainly fits for when she met the 'A' she refers to in her diary, and both families are from Munich. It shouldn't be hard to find out if they knew each other."

"Oh, we're going to know in the next few minutes, believe me. But back to my original point. These people have no power. There's no way they arranged the murder of the corporal."

Stadler agreed. "And how would they have known the corporal had pulled their file?"

"There are only three people who definitely knew."

Stadler glanced at him, then returned his attention to the file. "You mean Corporal Friedel, and Mr. and Mrs. Dettman?"

"Exactly."

"Well, obviously, Friedel didn't order his own murder, so you're suggesting that one of the Dettmans did?"

"There's only one Dettman who could do that."

Stadler held up the hand-written note from Corporal Friedel. "It says here that Mr. Dettman wasn't aware that Mrs. Dettman had requested the file a week earlier. Doesn't that suggest the corporal told him about her request?"

Vogel's head slowly bobbed. "If he found out his wife requested the file, how would he have reacted?"

"Well, the fact he requested the file and she did the same a week before, means they both lied to us when we asked them if they knew who 'A' might be."

"Agreed."

"And the fact he requested the file the same day we questioned them, suggests it was the first time Arland as a suspect had occurred to him. The fact his wife had requested it a week before means she had somehow become aware of who 'A' was."

"Exactly. The question is, how did she find out?"

"It has to be the diary. We know there must have been a diary in her nightstand, and that it was most likely written in Friday evening before Annie went to meet Arland, and it's now missing. If the mother was the one who removed it, she very well might have found it long before that."

Vogel was impressed with his underling's reasoning. "If she found out about Arland from the diary, and she requested the file a week ago, she must have done so to confirm who 'A' might be. She obviously suspected it was Arland because she requested the file by name, but she was probably trying to find out if he was in Munich still, or was now in Berlin."

"But if she found out, why didn't she confront her daughter?"

"Maybe she did."

Stadler looked him askance. "What do you mean?"

"Well, maybe she did. Does that file show when it was actually delivered to Dettman's office?"

Stadler flipped back to the front page. "Thursday."

"So, let's assume she found out Thursday. She has to figure out what to do. Her daughter was likely referring to her secret rendezvous plan for Friday night. She returns home from work, heads out to meet Arland, her mother follows her, confronts her, and in her rage, murders her."

Stadler slumped in his seat, the file dropping to his lap. "So, she really did murder her own daughter." He shook his head. "That could explain Corporal Friedel's murder. Her husband finds out what his wife has done, and realizes the only connection between her and Arland is this file request, and the only person who would know about the request would be the corporal. He calls in a favor, and has the corporal eliminated to protect his wife."

Vogel sighed. "The theory does seem to fit the facts, but there's one hole in it."

"What's that?"

"We know that the murder didn't happen right away. Annie and Arland were in that apartment for some time before she was murdered."

"How do you know that? They're young, maybe they just jumped in bed right away. And if it was his first time, well, you know, bing bang boom, it's done."

Vogel wagged a finger. "You're forgetting one thing."

"What's that?"

"They ate the food and drank the wine she brought with her. That takes time. That's a romantic evening that ended in lovemaking. If her mother were so desperate to save her daughter's virtue, why wouldn't she have charged in right away and stopped the event before it happened? Why would she wait, possibly hours, before coming in after the fact, if it were so important to her? If it were so important that she save her daughter's virtue so they could continue with their plans to marry her off and secure their future, why would she risk it by waiting?"

Stadler stared at him. "You're right, it makes no sense." He smiled slightly. "But I bet you have a theory."

"I have lots of guesses. She might have stood outside debating what to do, finally coming to a decision. She might have gone to tell her husband what was happening, then brought him back, and one or both of them committed the murder."

"He seemed genuinely shocked though when we informed him."

Vogel agreed. "If she did leave to tell him, she changed her mind and came back to deal with the situation herself." He sighed. "We don't have enough information yet." He jabbed a finger at the file still sitting in Stadler's lap. "But that's the biggest breakthrough we've had. If Arland isn't the murderer, he had to have been in the room when the murder occurred."

"But if he is the murderer, do you really think he's going to be sitting at home?"

Vogel shrugged. "We're about to find out."

Wilhelmine Ring Residential District

Berlin, Nazi Germany

Arland sat on the edge of a stone fountain, the apartment building his family had called home for the past six months visible at the end of the street. He wanted justice for Annie, yet he still wasn't sure how to achieve it. The entire truth had to come out. The police had to know everything, but it would only be his word against everyone else's. There were too many people involved, and every one of them was guilty, and he wanted them all brought to justice. The very notion he might be the only one to pay, disgusted him, but he had been racking his brain for almost two days on how to accomplish his goals, and had failed miserably in figuring out a solution. The only thing he could think of now was to turn himself in and pray that whoever interrogated him was interested in the whole truth, rather than just a quick arrest.

A vehicle raced down the street, coming to a halt directly in front of the fountain. He gulped as four uniformed police officers climbed out of the car. One of them scanned the area, his eyes coming to rest on him. The officer pointed at him.

"You! Go home or get out of here, I don't care which."

Arland jumped to his feet and sprinted away. He ducked into an alley and stopped, his heart hammering at the close call. He should keep running, but he had to know why the police were here. He poked his head around the corner and watched as another car pulled up, two plain-clothes men stepping out. He recognized them as those who had arrived at Annie's house yesterday, and it could mean only one thing.

They had figured out he was involved, that his family was involved.

And a smile spread at the thought justice might finally prevail.

Nicklas Residence, Wilhelmine Ring Residential District

Berlin, Nazi Germany

Vogel rushed up the stairs with the others, his chest pounding with excitement. This was the most significant break in the case so far. There was little doubt Arland Nicklas was the 'A' referred to in the diary, and though he doubted they would find the young man sitting at home with his family, they would at least finally get some answers as to what might have been the motive behind the murder.

They reached the door and Vogel pointed at either end of the hallway, an officer taking up position at each stairwell to make sure no one came onto the floor and got in the way. He hammered his fist on the door. "Kriminalpolizei! Open the door at once!" He banged again, then tried the doorknob. It was locked. "Kriminalpolizei! This is your last warning! Open the door at once!"

He stepped back and tilted his head toward the door. Stadler stepped forward and with one swift kick had the cheap door buckling. Vogel put a shoulder into it, finishing it off, and everyone charged inside, weapons drawn. He found Arland's parents, Alexander and Karin, huddled in the far corner of the living room holding each other, terrified.

Stadler and the two officers headed down the hallway to search the home as Vogel trained his weapon on the parents. "Where is Arland?"

"H-he's not here," said Alexander. "Wh-what's this all about?"

"He's wanted for the murder of Annie Dettman."

Alexander's eyes shot wide. "Annie? She's dead?"

"You knew her?"

Stadler and the others re-emerged, shaking their heads. "He's not here, sir."

Vogel returned his attention to the parents, lowering his weapon. "How do you know Annie?"

"Our families were good friends in Munich. They moved here about six years ago and we lost touch." Alexander's face paled. "You think our son murdered her?"

"We know he was with her Friday night when she was murdered. If you know where he is, you'd best tell us."

Alexander shook his head. "I'm sorry, but I haven't seen my son."

"Since when?"

His shoulders slumped. "Since Friday."

"And what about you?" Vogel asked Karin.

"I haven't seen him either."

"Sir."

Vogel turned toward one of the officers standing near the fireplace mantel. He pointed at a family photo.

"I just saw this boy."

Vogel stepped over and grabbed the picture. He held it up to the parents. "Is this your son? Is this Arland?"

They both nodded.

"Where did you see him?" he asked the officer.

"Just at the end of the street. He was sitting at a fountain when we arrived. I ordered him to go home or leave the area."

Vogel handed the photo back. "Put in the call. I want everyone in the area looking for this boy."

"Yes, sir." The officer rushed out of the apartment.

Vogel stepped closer to the parents. "If you know where he might be hiding, now is the time to tell me, otherwise he might just get himself shot."

Karin stepped forward, pressing her hands against Vogel's chest, staring up at him as tears flowed. "Please, you've got it all wrong. My son didn't kill Annie. I swear he didn't."

"I'm sorry, ma'am, but your word isn't enough."

She shook her head. "No, you don't understand. I know he didn't kill her, because I did!"

Dettman Residence

Berlin, Nazi Germany

Dettman sat at his desk, waiting for confirmation the favor called in had been completed. He had been sick to his stomach from the moment he had hung up the phone. He had finally become one of them.

He was finally a true Nazi.

He could never have imagined he would order the death of an innocent person simply to protect himself. What he had done was shameful, and his indoctrination was now complete. He had always prided himself on never taking a bribe and staying above the fray by never calling in a favor, never profiting from his position. He enjoyed the respect and the power it had given him. He had enjoyed the new lifestyle it had provided, though that had worn off over time.

He didn't like having servants. It reminded him too much of how his wife had once toiled, cleaning the houses of the very type of people they had now become. He kept a minimal staff, bringing in extra when necessary, and treated them with respect. The only time he could recall truly being angry was when the gardener's young assistant had ogled his Annie in a private moment. He showed no quarter, nor would any father.

His wife, on the other hand, too often treated the staff with disdain, and he wondered if she had learned these bad habits from the people she had once served, and if she had, it crushed his soul to think of what she had gone through for so many years because he hadn't earned enough income to provide for the family.

But none of that mattered now.

There were no innocents.

His wife had murdered her own daughter, and to protect her, he had ordered the murder of Corporal Friedel, a young man who had served him loyally and capably for the past two years. He was now no longer a Nazi in name only.

He was a murderer like the rest of them.

He eyed the phone, wondering if it was too late to call it off. Yet letting Friedel live meant his wife would hang. He sighed. Part of him didn't believe life was worth living anymore. The woman he had married was long gone, and it broke his heart, yet it was his fault. When the young Nicklas girl, Gabriele, had drowned, questions were asked, uncomfortable questions, and he was forced to take action to protect his daughter and the family.

He had made a call much like the one today, and had been given a job in Berlin with far more responsibility than he deserved. It was his membership ID number that trumped any qualification requirement. They had fled Munich and the questions, the suspicions, and settled into their new life, leaving the past behind them. And apparently, after all this time, it had finally caught up to them, and as he had feared it would all those years ago, it had destroyed his family.

The phone rang and he grabbed the receiver, pressing it to his ear. "This is Dettman."

"The job is done."

Bile filled his mouth as his stomach flipped. He grabbed his forehead, massaging his temples. "Understood," he finally managed to say. The call ended and he hung the phone up, slumping in his chair.

"What have I become?" he muttered. He eyed the drawer containing his sidearm. There was an easy way out of this. What did he have to live for? His daughter was dead, his wife was a murderer, and now so was he. Despite how much he loved his wife, she deserved to be executed for her crime. He couldn't even look at her now, and he wasn't sure he ever could again. She had become a beast, a vile creature that didn't deserve his love, or his devotion.

Or his protection.

His eyes burned as he stared at the family photo on his desk. He picked it up, pressing his thumb against his wife's face, removing her from the memory, instead focusing on his smiling daughter, standing beside him in a pretty dress she had been so proud to wear.

"Oh, Annie, I'm so sorry!" he cried. He reached for the drawer and pulled it open. The weapon sat there in its holster, beckoning him, promising deliverance from the hell that was now his life.

The phone rang again, startling him. He reached for it, then hesitated, staring at the gun and the relief it could provide. He sighed, closing his eyes. He grabbed the phone. "This is Dettman."

"Sorry to disturb you at this hour, sir. This is Major Ostwald. I'm afraid I have some disturbing news."

Dettman was well aware of what the disturbing news would be, yet played ignorant. "What is it?"

"I'm afraid Corporal Friedel has been murdered, sir."

"Murdered? By whom? How?" He trusted his reaction would allay anyone's suspicions he might be involved.

"He was shot in the head at his desk, sir. We don't know who did it. A suspect was seen fleeing the building, but beyond a general description, we don't know who he was."

"Is there any indication as to why?"

"No, sir. There's no evidence that anything is missing from your office, or that there was even a search of it. We believe the killer entered, shot the corporal, then left."

"I'm on my way."

"Yes, sir."

Dettman hung up the phone then eyed the still open drawer with his weapon. He sighed and slammed it shut then rose. He debated changing his clothes, but that would mean going to the bedroom and risking an encounter with his wife. He didn't trust what he might do to her, and at the moment, he couldn't care less if he ever saw her again.

He straightened himself in the full-length mirror on the wall behind the door, and as he was about to leave, the phone rang yet again. He exhaled loudly, then stepped back to his desk, picking up the receiver. "This is Dettman."

"Sir, there's something you need to know."

He didn't recognize the voice. "Who is this?"

"A friend in the Party."

He stood a little straighter, his heart rate picking up a few extra beats. "Yes?"

"They've just arrested your daughter's murderer."

His jaw dropped and his eyes shot wide. "What?"

"She was just picked up a few minutes ago."

He turned toward the closed door, wondering if he could have possibly missed the sounds of an arrest downstairs while lost in his own sorrow and self-hatred. "Who is it?"

"A woman named Karin Nicklas."

His legs became unsteady, and he braced himself against the desk at the naming of the murderer.

Arland's mother.

And then everything became clear. It all made sense. His mind raced as he struggled to maintain control, his emotions threatening to overwhelm him.

"Where are they taking her?"

"To the Kriminalpolizei headquarters."

He picked up Vogel's card, sitting on his desk, and read off the address.

"Yes, sir, that's it."

"Very well, thank you."

He ended the call and his entire body shook at the horrible mistake he had made. His wife wasn't the murderer. She was innocent. He collapsed in his chair, confused.

Why would she confess to the murder? What possible purpose could it serve? Bile filled his mouth at a sudden realization.

If his wife was innocent, then Corporal Friedel never needed to die.

Dettman Residence

Berlin, Nazi Germany

Johanna Dettman lay on the bed, curled into a sobbing ball. She gripped her pillow, staring at the family photo on her nightstand. Her daughter was dead, and her husband wouldn't speak to her. She thought yesterday was the worst day of her life, finding out her daughter had been murdered, but today, imagining what her husband thought of her and her involvement, was crushing. The door to the bedroom opened and her heart leaped. She spun her head to see her husband standing in the doorway.

She rolled upright. "I'm so sorry."

He said nothing, instead closing the door. He stepped over to the bed and sat beside her, then wrapped his arms around her, holding her tight. She hugged him back, hard, and they both sobbed in each other's arms, saying nothing. He finally inhaled deeply and pulled away, staring into her eyes.

"I just got a phone call. They arrested Karin Nicklas for the murder of Annie."

Johanna's jaw dropped. "Oh, no!"

He eyed her. "What do you mean, 'Oh, no?'"

"I mean that's terrible." She eyed him. "Wait, what's going on here?"

"I thought you had murdered our daughter."

She nearly fainted at his words, and it took her a moment to regain control. "How could you possibly think that?"

"Because of what you said."

"But you never let me finish!"

He squared his shoulders, staring at her. "Tell me everything."

"Well, when I found she was meeting Arland for her rendezvous, I followed her with every intention of stopping what was going on, but I became frightened, because I couldn't be sure of Arland's motives. How he could possibly be in love with our daughter simply made no sense, not after what had happened to Gabriele."

He frowned. "Yes, I was wondering that too."

"So, I feared for her safety and for mine, so I left with the intention of getting you, but then I realized if you were to become involved and something were to happen, it could destroy your career and ruin all of our plans."

"What did you do?"

"I had the home address for them because of the file that Friedel had pulled, so I went there."

"You saw Karin?"

"Yes, and she was quite shocked to see me, let me tell you. I told her what was going on, and that whatever was happening between their son and our daughter had to be stopped. She flew into a rage, clearly disgusted at the notion he would be in a relationship with our daughter, and frankly, I don't blame her. I gave her the address and she said she would take care of it, then slammed the door in my face. I never would have thought she would do what she did."

Her husband sat there, staring blankly at her, finally responding. "What did you do then?"

"I came straight home. I had assumed she had stopped their plans and brought her son home, and that Annie stayed overnight to keep up the pretense she was staying with her girlfriends, and would return as planned so that we would be none the wiser. I never dreamed she was dead until you told me."

His shoulders slumped. "I wish you had come to me."

Tears filled her eyes once again and her head slumped to her chest. "I wish I had the courage to go in myself and stop them." She stared up at him. "What do we do now?"

"We have nothing to hide anymore. If questioned, we tell them the truth."

"Everything?"

"Everything. We tell them about the diaries, we tell them about you finding out, we tell them about you requesting the file, and we tell them about how our daughter, through her actions, killed Gabriele Nicklas."

Wilhelmine Ring Residential District

Berlin, Nazi Germany

Arland watched from his hiding place as his mother was pushed into the back of a police car, and his smile spread further. The police now knew his family was involved, and now, finally, the correct questions would be asked. Finally, he could get the rest and the closure he needed. When he had spotted Annie at Dieter Maier's party six months ago, he had been overjoyed. He had finally found his best friend that had disappeared so soon after the tragedy of his sister's death. They had spoken at length that night, and he swore he fell in love with her with the first crack of her smile.

They had seen each other frequently after that, always in secret because of her parents' plans for her future. And as they had grown closer and fallen more deeply in love, they had begun to make plans. Running away was something difficult in today's Germany, but it was possible with the right amount of money and the right connections. He had little opportunity to earn because his family desperately needed every *pfennig* that he could bring in. She, on the other hand, didn't need her paycheck, so she was saving her money, and also asking her parents for extra every time she could, using the excuse of wanting to buy something that might make her more attractive to a future mate. Their disgusting plans for her had them eating it up, handing money over whenever asked. She would return home with some new article of clothing or some bauble, having paid half of what she claimed.

But money was only half the picture.

She was listening. She was listening to everything. Her parents assumed she showed no interest in anything to do with her father's job, but that was merely a pretense so she could sit in the room and listen to unfiltered conversations her parents presumed were ignored. Sometimes, she would even sit in her father's office, reading a book while he worked. He loved spending every moment he could with her, and welcomed her company.

And she would listen.

And over the months, she had gathered enough dirt on the right people that they would be able to get the papers they needed to cross the border into Switzerland. It was only a matter of time before they escaped so they could start their own life together. But that had all changed the night his mother had barged in the apartment as they lay there, naked in bed. That had all changed the night the truth about Annie had been revealed to him.

And that had been the night justice was finally delivered to the woman he loved, to the woman who had destroyed his family, to the woman responsible for the death of his sweet innocent sister.

Kriminalpolizei Headquarters

Prinz-Albrecht Straße, Berlin, Nazi Germany

Vogel stared at the woman who had confessed to the murder of Annie Dettman. After Karin Nicklas had blurted out her confession, he had told her to keep her mouth shut. There were too many witnesses to what she was about to say, and with a senior Nazi Party official involved, he had to be careful what was revealed in front of others. Stadler stood in his customary corner behind the woman, who sat fidgeting in her chair.

Vogel took out his pad and pen. "You said you murdered Annie Dettman."

"No, that's not what I said."

Vogel tensed as a pit of rage formed. If this woman had given a false confession to give her son time to escape, he would make sure she was punished to the fullest extent of the law for wasting his precious time. "We all heard you confess to the murder. Now you're saying you didn't kill her?"

"Oh, I killed her, but I didn't murder her."

His eyes narrowed. "I fail to see the distinction."

"Murder is wrong. Killing someone who's guilty of killing another, isn't. That's justice."

"Justice? Justice for what?"

"For the death of my little girl, Gabriele."

Vogel leaned back, relaxing slightly. "Tell me."

"Our daughter died six years ago. My husband and I had taken Arland to see a doctor about his asthma. We left our daughter at home with Annie. Annie was thirteen at the time, and our daughter was only six. Annie apparently fell asleep on the couch, and our daughter went outside to feed the ducks at the river. She fell in the water and got tangled in the reeds. A neighbor found her, but she was already dead. He cut her loose and brought her back to the house where he found Annie sleeping. The Dettmans used their connections to get themselves moved, and to make sure the investigation never involved the name of their daughter. The official ruling was accidental death by drowning, and that no one was to blame. But it was Annie's fault. We left our poor innocent girl in her care, and she instead shirked her responsibilities and decided to take a nap. If she had only stayed awake, our daughter never would have left the house, and our daughter would be alive today. But instead, Annie escaped justice, not because she was innocent, but because of who her father was. There was nothing we could do about it."

Vogel leaned back, folding his arms. They finally had a motive that made sense. Revenge. "Tell me how you found out about the relationship."

"Johanna told me."

Vogel exchanged a quick glance with Stadler, his underling clearly surprised at the revelation, as was he. "Tell me what happened."

"Friday evening, she came to our door in quite the state. Needless to say, I was shocked to see her after all these years."

"This was the first time you had seen her since the death of your daughter?"

"I didn't even know they were in Berlin. If I had, I would have sought them out and killed Annie six months ago."

"She came to your door. Then what?"

"She told me that my son and her daughter were in a relationship, and that they were together in an apartment, intending to sin."

"Are you a religious woman?"

"I am. I don't believe in premarital sex, but I do believe in an eye for an eye. I lost my daughter because of theirs, so they should lose their daughter because of mine."

"So, she told you about their rendezvous. Then what?"

"She gave me the address, I said I'd take care of it, then I slammed the door in her ugly face."

"What did Mrs. Dettman do then?"

She shrugged. "I don't know, but I never saw her again. I assume she went home."

"And what did you do?"

"I got a knife from the kitchen drawer then went to the address she gave me. The door was unlocked. I heard them in the bedroom. I went in and I killed her. End of story."

"But it isn't the end, is it?"

"What do you mean?"

"You killed her. How did you kill her?"

"I told you. With my knife."

"Yes. But how did you use the knife?"

"What do you mean?"

"Did you stab her in the heart, did you slice open her stomach, what did you do?"

She stared at him blankly. "I don't remember."

"You remember everything else, but you don't remember how you actually killed her?"

She rubbed her thighs, staring about as if searching for something. She stopped, her face brightening. "No, I do! I stabbed her." She nodded firmly. "Yes, I stabbed her."

"Do you remember where you stabbed her?"

She motioned at her torso. "In this area. Once, twice. More. I was so angry, I don't know how many times I stabbed her. A lot."

"And that's it? You just stabbed her?"

Her eyes widened. "No, no. I cut her throat, too."

"Which came first?"

She shrugged. "Does it matter?"

"I'm just curious. I like to file a complete report whenever possible."

"Fine. I cut her throat then I stabbed her."

"Then what happened?"

"I left."

"And where was your son during all of this?"

"Standing in the corner, getting dressed, I think."

"He didn't try to stop you?"

"He knew better."

"Was he aware of Annie's involvement in his sister's death?"

"No, we kept the truth from him."

"Does he know now?"

"Yes. I told him why I did what I did."

"And how did he feel about that?"

"I don't know. He ran away. I haven't seen him since."

"After he ran off, what did you do?"

"I went home."

"There wasn't something else you did in the apartment?"

She shrugged. "I can't think of anything."

"You didn't clean up?"

She stared at him.

"Well?"

"Well what?"

"What did you do with her clothes, her purse, the wine, the food?"

She continued to stare at him. "I-I don't remember. I was in quite the state. I suppose I must have cleaned up any evidence that my son was there." She shook her head, staring at her hands. "I'm sorry, I'm not clear on what happened after I killed her. I wasn't thinking straight."

"Did you leave with your son?"

"Yes, *that* I remember."

"Do you remember if you locked the door when you left?"

"No, I told you it was unlocked."

"Right. So, you killed her, you cleaned up, then what?"

"We got outside and Arland ran off."

"Then what?"

"I went home."

"Where did you dispose of the items you took from the apartment?"

Another pause. "I don't remember. I must have thrown them somewhere."

Vogel frowned. "Did you tell your husband?"

"Of course not."

"Wasn't he curious as to where his son was?"

"Of course, but I wasn't about to tell him that his son had carried on a sinful affair with the person responsible for our daughter's death. It would crush him."

"And you have nothing else to tell me?"

"No."

"Then let me ask you this. Did you do anything to the body?"

"What do you mean?"

The door burst open and Dettman barged inside. His jaw dropped and his eyes shot wide as they settled on Karin Nicklas. "So, it *was* you!"

Vogel leaped to his feet, placing himself between the enraged father and the suspect. "Sir, you can't be in here."

"I have a right to confront my daughter's murderer."

"You have a right in court, sir, not here. We haven't charged her yet."

"Has she confessed?"

"Yes."

Dettman reached behind him and drew a weapon, swinging it around. Stadler jumped forward, shoving Vogel aside as a shot rang out. Stadler groaned and fell into Karin, knocking her from her chair and onto the floor. Vogel scrambled to his feet and leaped forward, grabbing the man by the wrist and redirecting the weapon as it fired twice more. Shouts erupted on the other side of the door and boots pounded as he struggled with the large man.

Vogel glanced over his shoulder at his partner. "Otto, are you all right?"

"The bastard shot me," gasped Stadler, his voice strained.

The door flew open and two officers entered, their weapons drawn as Dettman wrenched his hand free and shoved Vogel to the side. He aimed at the twisted pile of Stadler and Karin. Vogel pulled his weapon and opened fire as the two officers did the same, and after the barrage of gunfire was over, Dettman collapsed to the floor, blood oozing from a dozen wounds.

A scream broke out at the doorway and Vogel spun toward the sound to see Johanna Dettman, horror written across her face, staring at her dying husband. "What have you done?" she cried as she rushed forward.

The officers grabbed her as Vogel secured Dettman's weapon. He waved them off and they let her go. She dropped to her knees and cradled her husband's head in her lap. "Why did you have to shoot him?" she cried. "He did nothing wrong!"

"No," Dettman gasped. "I deserve this. I…I gave the order to have Friedel killed."

She gasped in shock. "But why? Why would you do such a thing?"

"I thought I was protecting you…" A loud sigh followed his last words, and his eyes fluttered shut one final time, leaving Hermann Dettman to be judged not by society, but by God, for what he had done.

Charité University Hospital

Berlin, Nazi Germany

The surgeon emerged through the swinging doors. Vogel and the dozens of other detectives and uniformed officers that had held vigil these past hours, turned toward the man as one, for that's what they were.

They were one.

They were a single, cohesive brotherhood that always stood together no matter how intense the rivalries sometimes became. And though Stadler had made himself no friends, his selfless act hadn't gone unnoticed, nor had the fact that the young man's partner had remained at his side from the moment the incident had ended. As far as Vogel was concerned, Stadler had proven where his loyalties lay.

Vogel stepped forward. "How is he, Doctor?"

"Your friend got lucky. The bullet missed the descending thoracic aorta by less than half an inch. He's still lost a lot of blood, and his lung was slightly damaged. But we got the bullet out and stopped the bleeding. He should make a full recovery."

Vogel smiled broadly and extended a hand to the doctor who shook it as relief swept the room. "Thank you very much, Doctor. That young fool took a bullet for me."

"Maybe tell him next time to shoot before the other guy."

Everyone roared with laughter, the tension of these past hours finally relieved.

"When can I see him?"

"Not for a while. Come back in the morning." The doctor eyed the crowd of police. "Where's his family?"

"They're out of town. I've had word sent to them, so I would expect you'll see them in the morning."

"Very well. I have to get back to my patient." He turned and returned through the doors, receiving slaps on the back by the jubilant officers. Vogel checked his watch and cursed. It was 3:00 a.m. and he had an appointment in two and a half hours that couldn't be missed.

Nicklas Residence, Wilhelmine Ring Residential District

Berlin, Nazi Germany

Arland unlocked the door to his family's apartment. He slowly twisted the knob, cringing at every sound the mechanism made, never removing his eyes from the uniformed officer at the far end of the hall, sitting in the corner, sound asleep. He pushed open the door and stepped inside, closing it behind him. He creeped through the hallway and was surprised to find his father asleep in his chair rather than his bed. He sat across from him, then leaned forward and tapped his father's knee. The man stirred, his eyes opening in a squint, then he bolted upright.

"Arland, where have you been?" His father jumped from the chair and wrapped his arms around him, hugging him tight. Shocked, Arland wasn't sure how to react at first, and then felt himself melting. All the anger bottled up inside toward the man washed away, and he grabbed on, returning the embrace. His shoulders shook.

"Why didn't you tell me? Why didn't you tell me she killed my sister?"

"We were protecting you." His father pushed him gently away, returning to his chair. "She was your best friend, and what she had done was foolish and irresponsible, but it wasn't intentional. She never meant for your sister to die. She was just tired and fell asleep. Yes, your sister would be alive today if she hadn't, but you can hardly blame a child for the death of another child."

Arland bristled at the defense of the person who had murdered his sister. "I can't believe you're saying this. Mom understood. Annie was selfish and irresponsible. She was thirteen. She knew better. The only reason she wasn't punished was because of who her father was. He protected her by taking the family here so she could escape the consequences of her actions. And you and mom kept this a secret! You saw what it was doing to Mom. She's never been the same. It destroyed her! If she had been able to confront Annie and her parents, the things that needed to be said would have been said. Maybe she would've got some closure, maybe she could've moved on. But instead, she was robbed of that chance. You should've heard her when she found us. The rage was unlike anything I have ever seen. It was as if she were reliving that day, all that pain and sorrow. It was as if she's always been reliving that day, every day, waiting for her chance to finally exorcise the demons that had been tormenting her for six years. Now that Annie's been found, now that the truth has been revealed, my sister can finally rest in peace, and Mom can finally find hers!"

His father stared at him, slowly shaking his head. "You don't understand what's happened. Our family has been destroyed once again. They've arrested your mother for murdering Annie. She'll be put to death for sure. All I have left is you, and I fear you've played some part in this that will have you lost to me as well."

Arland's chest tightened with an ache almost as great as when his mother had revealed the truth to him about how Gabriele had died, and who was responsible. He rose and headed out the door, his father calling after him. He walked up to the sleeping officer and kicked his boots. The man awoke and scrambled to his feet.

"I'm Arland Nicklas. I believe you're looking for me."

Luft Family Grocery

Berlin, Nazi Germany

Vogel stood in the grocery, Manfred Luft near the rear door as they waited for the delivery of black market goods by Drake Pankow, the man Luft had called to report what that daft bat Ingrid had said about Sofia. There was a coded knock and Vogel drew his weapon as Luft, trembling, looked at him. Vogel gave a single nod and stepped out of sight.

Luft opened the door. "Good morning."

"Mr. Luft, how are we this fine day?"

"Very good. Very good."

"We have a delivery for you."

Jars and cans rattled as Luft walked past him with a crate filled with hard-to-come-by items. Another man walked by, his jaw flapping as he ran down the inventory of items. Vogel stepped from his hiding place and glanced down the hallway toward the door. It was closed, the man evidently making his delivery alone.

Luft and Pankow placed their crates on the floor as Vogel cleared his throat, his pistol aimed directly at the black marketeer. The man spun around, reaching behind his back.

"Please give me an excuse."

Pankow smiled, raising his hands. "Not, I think, today."

Vogel jerked his chin at Luft. "Get his weapon." A trembling Luft did so. "Bring it to me."

A moment later, the weapon was in his hand. He stuffed it in his pocket. "Do you know who I am?"

"No, but I have a feeling you don't know who I am."

Vogel smirked. "Your name is Drake Pankow, and you're a nobody."

Pankow glanced over his shoulder at Luft. "Have you been talking out of turn?"

Luft shook his head rapidly. "No! Never!"

Vogel stepped closer. "My name is Kriminalinspektor Vogel. Now do you know who I am?"

The man's eyes widened slightly as his mouth opened. "Ah, the husband of Sofia Vogel."

"Yes. And I only want to know one thing. Who sent the man who accosted my wife?"

Gruber Residence

Berlin, Nazi Germany

It had turned out that Pankow wasn't as tough as he wanted others to believe. The moment Vogel had pulled his baton, Pankow's employer had been revealed, and it was a man he had dealt with in the past. Felix Gruber. Gruber was scum, the rotund son of a senior Nazi Party official. He flouted the law with impunity. There was no touching him. The best the police could hope for, was to catch those who worked for the man in the act, and hurt his operation, but they could never bring it to an end. Yet Gruber had to know there was a delicate balance that needed to be maintained, and going after a police officer's family was not the way to do so.

Vogel had Pankow by the collar, his Luger pressed into the bastard's ribcage as he kicked on the door of Gruber's luxurious residence. The door opened, one of Gruber's henchmen glaring at him. "Do you have any idea what time it is?"

"It's time to get your boss up. Tell him Kriminalinspektor Vogel is here on urgent business, and he won't want to make me wait for him."

The man frowned but let them inside, closing the door behind them. "Stay here." He headed up a set of stairs, then returned several minutes later. "He'll be right down."

They were shown into Gruber's office, a room Vogel had just recently been in when he had asked a favor of the criminal. Unfortunately, that transaction meant Vogel owed the man, yet none of that mattered today. He shoved Pankow into a chair then sat in another, still aiming his weapon at Pankow.

Vogel was exhausted. He had been running on adrenaline for hours, and he was crashing. He needed to go home and get some rest so he could think clearly, but not until this business was done.

The door opened and Gruber entered in a bathrobe, clearly not pleased. Vogel didn't bother rising, for no respect was deserved.

"Kriminalinspektor Vogel, what could possibly be so important that you would interrupt my day at such an hour?" Gruber dropped in his chair behind his ornate desk, the leather clad furniture groaning under his substantial frame.

Vogel tilted his head toward Pankow. "Yesterday, someone under your employ accosted my wife, pressing a knife against her throat in front of my children, and told her to tell me to back off on an investigation into the black market that I'm not conducting."

Gruber stared at Pankow for a moment, and the man cringed before he returned his gaze to Vogel. "Of course you wouldn't investigate a black market operation. You investigate homicides. I'm well aware of that fact, and since you know this, you must know I had nothing to do with what happened.”

“Yes. When he told me who he worked for, I realized that was the case.”

Gruber growled. “Then why are you here, wasting my time?”

“Because I’m telling you right now, to your face so he hears it, that if anyone threatens my family again, I won’t rest until your entire organization is brought down, and I don’t give a damn who your father is.” Vogel jabbed a finger at Gruber. “And I want the same message delivered to the piece of shit who held a knife to my wife’s throat in front of my children, terrorizing them. You tell him, that if I ever hear of him doing this again to anyone, his days are numbered.”

Gruber regarded him, saying nothing, though the flaring of his nostrils clearly suggested he was furious. He wasn’t used to being talked to this way, the fear of who his father was usually enough to keep anyone in his presence well-mannered.

And it was another reason Vogel needed rest.

He was being foolish.

Gruber exhaled loudly, a smile spreading. “Inspector, you have my word, no one under my employ will ever bother your family again, and rest assured, a most persuasive lesson in threat delivery will be administered to not only our friend here, but to whoever he had accost your wife.”

Vogel stood. “Then our business here is done.” He turned for the door, then paused. “Oh, and I don’t want anything happening to Mr.

Luft. He was well aware that I was about to beat him to within an inch of his life if he didn't tell me what I wanted to know."

"Of course, Mr. Luft is innocent in this."

Vogel left Gruber's house and climbed back in his car, his eyes drooping now that the threat to his family had been eliminated. Yes, Gruber could go back on his word, but now that the man was aware that Vogel, and therefore likely others at police headquarters, knew what had occurred, he wouldn't dare do anything.

It was why what Pankow had done was such a foolish act.

Vogel arrived home quickly enough, and dragged his ass up the stairs to his apartment. A neatly wrapped package was sitting in front of the door, his title and name written in large print, reminding anyone who might think to steal it that it belonged to a police detective. In this building, however, everyone was well aware of who he was and what he did, so there was little chance of it being stolen by a resident.

He picked it up and smiled, the weight and size confirming what it was. He unlocked the door and stepped inside. Ingrid was nowhere to be found, and he assumed his wife had sent her home. He checked on the children, finding them still asleep in their bedroom. He opened the door to the master bedroom and found his wife sitting up, sipping a cup of tea, eating some toast.

He smiled. "Well, I'm happy to see I didn't wake you. How are you feeling?"

She shrugged. "All right, I guess. I just sent Ingrid home a few minutes ago. What did you say to her?"

"Nothing that shouldn't have been said years ago."

She frowned. "I hope you didn't ruin my friendship with her. She can be quite the bother, but I do love her so."

"Don't worry, I'll go see her later today and apologize, but I've taken care of the problem. You've got nothing to worry about from now on."

She put down her cup. "Please tell me you didn't do anything stupid."

"If you mean, did I force Manfred Luft to reveal who his contact was under threat of a severe beating, then caught that man, threatened him with the same beating, then visited his employer, a well-known vicious black marketeer whose father is a senior Nazi, and threatened his entire operation if he didn't back off, then I don't think you want to know the answer."

Her eyes were wide. "Please tell me that's not what happened!"

He smiled. "See, I knew you wouldn't want to know." He sat on the edge of the bed, still gripping the package. "All you need to know is that we've come to an agreement, and you and the kids will never be threatened again by these people, and Mr. Luft won't be touched either."

Her shoulders slumped. "Thank God. We still have to live in this neighborhood." She finally noticed the package he was carrying. "What's that?"

He grinned, handing it to her. "Open it."

She eagerly tore away the paper wrapping the box. She opened the folded lid then her eyes shot wide as delight spread across her face. "My gramophone! Did you have it fixed?"

"Yes, at least I hope so. I haven't had a chance to try it."

She stared at him, tears of joy welling in her eyes. "But Wolfgang, we can't afford this."

He patted her leg. "Don't worry about it. It didn't cost us anything. I interviewed a young witness on Saturday, and it turns out he's a bit of a tinkerer, so I asked him if he would mind giving it a look for me. He agreed. I took it from the closet Sunday morning when I left, and dropped it off on my way to work. I guess he was able to fix it."

She wrapped her arms around the box. "Thank you so much. I've missed my music. It helps pass the day while you're away."

"When I get home, maybe we'll dance like we used to."

She smiled and her eyes glistened. "I miss that more than the music."

He leaned forward and kissed her, then rolled onto the other side of the bed. "I just need a few minutes."

And in less than that, he was sound asleep.

Charlottenstraße, Berlin, Nazi Germany

The phone call that had woken Vogel had delivered two critical pieces of information. One was that Arland Nicklas had turned himself in, and the other, perhaps just as crucial, was whose fingerprint was on the spare key to Emilia Schmitt's apartment—and it wasn't Arland or his mother. It was the biggest hole in Karin Nicklas' confession. Every detail she had given fit the crime and was corroborated by the evidence, except for one thing.

She said she had closed the door behind her and hadn't locked it. That might be fine, however, it left a question unanswered.

Who had returned the key?

Whoever had, should be the last one to have touched it, and just by the nature of how a key was held to lock a door, a fingerprint should have been left behind. Yes, there could have been overlapping fingerprints, and that would actually be expected, but in this case, there was only one. And while there were numerous explanations as to why, he had his suspicions.

He knocked on the door of Petra Berkner's apartment. He heard footsteps then the door was opened. The young woman's eyes shot wide. "Kriminalinspektor Vogel, was it? How can I help you?"

"I apologize for the early hour, however I have some questions for you that can't wait."

She stepped aside, holding the door open. "Of course, come in."

He entered the apartment and stepped into the living area to find Emilia Schmitt standing there. "Miss Schmitt, how are you doing?"

She shrugged. "A little better, I guess. I haven't been back to the apartment yet. The cleaner is supposed to be there later today."

"Good. Hopefully, you'll soon be able to put this behind you. You should be aware that we have a suspect in custody who's confessed to the crime. However, her confession has raised some other questions."

He motioned for them to sit down and they did. He took a seat opposite them. "I believe someone in this room isn't telling me the truth."

Emilia's eyebrows shot up. "I can assure you, every word I told you was true! I would never lie to the police."

Vogel turned to Petra. "And you? Would you lie to the police?"

Petra shifted uncomfortably in a way one didn't need to be a trained police officer to notice.

Emilia's jaw dropped. "Petra, did you lie?"

Petra trembled. She finally nodded, bursting into tears.

"Did you kill Annie?"

Vogel waved a hand in front of him. "No, no, your friend didn't kill anyone."

"Is that true?"

Petra clasped her friend's hands. "I could never kill anyone, you know that!"

Vogel leaned forward. "Why don't you tell us what happened?"

She wiped her tears away with the back of her hand and took a deep breath. "The next morning when the key wasn't there—"

"But you said it was!" interrupted Emilia.

"I'm sorry, but it wasn't. I grew a little concerned, so I went downstairs to check on her to make sure everything was all right. I was afraid perhaps her mystery lover had taken advantage of her, then once he had what he wanted, had left her an emotional wreck. I went down and knocked. There was no answer, so I tried the door. It was unlocked, so I went inside and I found..." Her voice cracked. "I found Annie."

Emilia gasped. "Why didn't you call the police?"

"Because I thought maybe I might get blamed, and you know who her father is. He could have me killed! I gave her the key without Emilia's permission. I was the one who had made it all possible."

"Then what did you do?" asked Vogel.

"I took everything. I took all of her clothes and her purse, anything that could identify her from the bedroom, then I cleaned up all the evidence that it had been a romantic interlude. I wanted it to look like rape and murder so there was no reason to suspect my involvement. I gathered everything up, locked the door, then hid the stuff in an alleyway a couple of apartment buildings down the street. I came home and prayed nobody found out, but when you knocked on my door Saturday morning and Emilia was with you, I remembered that I would be the only one who had a key to let anyone into the apartment, so I decided I had to tell at least part of the truth. I'm so ashamed of what I did. It's been eating me up inside." She sighed. "Frankly, I'm relieved you're here." She stared at him. "Am I in trouble?"

Vogel regarded the woman. She had lied, and those lies had affected their investigation, though in the end they had their murderer, and a confession. Now that the inconsistencies in Karin's story had been cleared up, he was confident the confession was solid enough for prosecution. The key hadn't been returned, Petra had taken it, and Karin's confusion over who had cleaned the apartment was now explained. He smiled slightly. "Probably, but not serious trouble. You panicked, and people are apt to do that in these situations. In the end, I think we have our killer. I'll talk to the prosecutor and see what we can figure out."

"Thank you," she murmured.

"One last question."

"Yes?"

"What did you do with the knife?"

"The knife?"

"The murder weapon. What did you do with it?"

Her eyes were wide as she shook her head. "I never saw it. It wasn't there."

Kriminalpolizei Headquarters

Prinz-Albrecht Straße, Berlin, Nazi Germany

Vogel strode into headquarters, yawning, only getting a couple of hours' rest before the phone had rung with word that Arland Nicklas had turned himself in. He had been placed in an interrogation room with two officers watching him, and the interrogation was now waiting on him.

And Abel was behind his desk once again.

"You should just move in, Sergeant. I think you spend more time here than you do at home."

Abel gave him a look. "Have you and my wife been talking? She said the same damn thing to me last night."

Vogel laughed. "It's her fault for marrying somebody so dedicated to their job."

Abel smiled. "So, what you're saying is it's her fault?"

Vogel grinned. "Exactly. Any word on Stadler?"

"I just got a call from one of our guys. They're taking shifts at the hospital. His parents arrived less than half an hour ago."

"And his condition?"

"Up until they arrived, improving. Now that they're there, who the hell knows with a father like that?"

Vogel grunted. "Yeah, I'm beginning to get a better picture of my young partner, and I think he might be a little misunderstood."

"Yesterday, I wouldn't have given the young man the time of day if it were up to me, but any man who would put himself in the path of a bullet to save his partner, is all right in my books."

"On that we agree, Sergeant." Vogel removed his jacket and hat as he headed into the detective pool. He hung them up, then sat at his desk, a pile of messages and reports waiting for him. He wanted to go into this interview fully aware of everything that had happened. A lot of irons were in the fire over the past two days, and as he leafed through the pile on his desk, much of what he expected was confirmed. No knife was missing from Emilia Schmitt's apartment, nor was there any evidence that a knife had been cleaned. This matched up with Karin Nicklas' claim that she had brought the knife with her, and Petra Berkner's assertion she hadn't found one when she cleaned the crime scene.

Emilia had also confirmed to an officer that she had given the apartment a thorough cleaning before she had left, a week before the murder, which again suggested that the stray hair they had found was indeed from the third person and, according to Naumann at the Medical Examiner's office, it matched a sample taken from Karin. This seemed to rule out any involvement by Johanna Dettman, as expected.

As he scanned Johanna's statement taken after the death of her husband, it tied up a lot of loose ends about the diaries, about her request for the file, her confirmation in their daughter's involvement in the death of Karin's daughter Gabriele, of the family's move to escape the scandal, and of her going to Karin's apartment and telling her where their children were and what they were about to do. It all matched up perfectly with Karin's story.

He skipped any reports that were interviews with attendees of Dieter Maier's party. None of that mattered now, since they had identified Arland. The forensics report on the clothes and wine bottle they had discovered revealed nothing beyond that the bottle of wine was extremely expensive, which confirmed that it was indeed the one Annie had stolen from her parents' wine cellar. And the clothes had been confirmed by a staff member to belong to Annie.

He rubbed his eyes, then rose and grabbed a cup of stale coffee. He downed it, then headed for the interrogation room. He opened the door and the two officers inside stood a little straighter. "I'll take it from here," he said as he sat down, spreading out the pertinent files, then readying his notepad and pen as the officers left, closing the door behind them.

"My name is Kriminalinspektor Vogel. I'm the lead detective investigating the murder of Annie Dettman. And your name is?"

"Arland Nicklas."

"Now, Arland, you turned yourself in this morning. I assume you have a reason for that."

"I do. I'm here to make sure justice is delivered."

"Then why don't you tell me what happened Friday?"

"I went to the address Annie had given me. She was already there. We ate some food and drank some wine that she had taken from her parents' house. Then we went to the bedroom and made love. It was the first time for both of us." He smiled, staring into the distance. "It was wonderful." His face clouded over. "Then my mother barged into the room and started screaming at me and screaming at her."

"What was she saying?"

"Stuff like, how could you do this? What are you doing? Don't you realize what she did? Stuff like that."

"And what had she done?

Arland's voice cracked. "She killed my sister."

"And how did that make you feel?"

He jerked upright in his chair. "How do you think it made me feel? Angry, disgusted, revolted, ashamed! I was in love with the murderer of my sister! I had just had sex with her! I had an entire future planned with the woman who had destroyed my family and destroyed my mother!"

"So, you just stood by while your mother murdered her?"

Arland stared at him for a moment, pursing his lips. "After I found out what Annie had done, what part she had played in the death of my sister, I couldn't care less what happened to her. There's no way I would have stopped anyone. She deserved to die, and I'm happy she's dead."

"You are aware that Annie was only thirteen years old, and she was only a child as well?"

"That's bullshit and you know it. When you're thirteen, you know better."

"Yes, you might know better, but you still make mistakes. Do you really think she deserved to die the way she did because of a mistake?"

"I only wish she hadn't been shown mercy. She died too quickly, as far as I'm concerned."

"Your mother testified she cut Annie's throat then stabbed her multiple times. She cleaned up the apartment to remove any evidence you had been there, and to make it more difficult to identify who Annie was, then she left and returned home, disposing of any incriminating evidence. Where did you go?"

"I just left."

Vogel regarded the young man, waiting for him to correct the account, but no correction came. "You left before your mother cleaned up, or with her?"

Arland stared at him, a slight smile spreading. "Do you really want the truth, Inspector?"

"That's why I'm here."

"I don't think you do, because then you'd have to admit you made a mistake. I heard them talking. Mr. Dettman's dead, and you shot him. His death is on you because you arrested my mother and let her confess to murder. If you hadn't arrested her, Dettman would still be alive. Annie told me how important he is, and how many people owe him favors. Do you really think your career is going to survive?"

Vogel faked disinterest by yawning heavily. The thought had occurred to him, of course, though he had concluded he would be safe, as Dettman wasn't nearly as important as he made himself out to be, and his attempts to marry off his daughter hadn't gone unnoticed, in fact, had gone unwelcomed, in the most senior of circles. "Your concern for my career is touching, however I'm quite certain I'll be just fine."

Arland smirked. "You have no idea, do you?"

"Why don't you enlighten me."

"You've arrested the wrong person. How do you think your superiors will react when they find out?"

Vogel leaned back, hiding his momentary shock, yet part of him wasn't surprised by the statement. He could understand Karin having trouble remembering the traumatic event of the murder, yet she had correctly detailed it eventually. But he had always had his doubts surrounding the cleanup. How she couldn't remember something such as that, had him wondering, yet he hadn't had time to pursue it after Dettman's interruption and subsequent death.

It wasn't until Petra confessed to being the one who had done the cleanup, that he finally had proof his doubts were correct, and as he had thought about the interview with Karin, he remembered he had prompted her with the details of the cleanup. She had merely used his own words to create a plausible story in a desperate attempt to make him believe her entire confession.

And if she had lied about the cleanup, then she could have been lying about the murder. She could have been protecting her son from the same fate her daughter had met.

Or was her son covering for her?

"Your mother was pretty convincing in her confession. Why don't you just tell me the truth."

"Brave man," said Arland, folding his arms. "Fine, I'll tell you. Everything happened exactly as I said, up to the point where she came in and started screaming. Once I found out the truth about Annie, about the part she had played in my sister's death, I didn't know what to think. Not only was she responsible for the death of my sister, she had lied to me. She had known what she had done, yet she had kept the truth from me for all these months when we were supposedly sharing each other's secrets, our deepest desires, all of our regrets and all of our dreams.

"And as she lay there in the bed, begging for forgiveness, something came over me. I took the knife from my mother and told her to leave the room, as I couldn't stand to look at her. I began questioning Annie on what had happened that day. And as I did so, I pictured my sister, dead, lying in her bed, her legs and hands still knotted by the reeds that had trapped her in the water, and I wanted Annie to feel what my sister had felt, the panic of knowing you were going to die, and that there's nothing you could do about it. I tied up her wrists and ankles with the bed sheets, then as I held a hand over her mouth, I called in my mother so she could watch Annie finally receive the justice she deserved. My mother tried to stop me, and she grabbed at my hand with the knife, begging me not to do it, not to throw away my own life, but I shoved her away.

"And then, as I stared into Annie's eyes, I slit her throat and watched the life drain from her, just as my sister's must have all those years ago. And when she finally gasped her last breath, and with my mother crying, 'What have you done, what have you done?' I felt a rage build in my heart at everything that had happened, of all the guilt everyone had been carrying, everyone except Annie.

"If it weren't for my asthma, we would never have gone to the doctor, my sister would never have been left alone with Annie, and she'd be alive today. If my parents had been more important, they might have been able to get justice for her at the time. If they hadn't tried to protect me, I would have known the truth all along. I would have known why I had lost my friend, rather than thinking it was something I had done. I was thirteen, I wasn't a fool. My friend disappeared, my best friend, yet she never wrote a single letter. I had always assumed I had done something wrong, something that had made her angry with me, and I had blamed myself for that for years. I blamed my mother for finally telling me the truth, but for doing it too late. If I had known, I never would have fallen in love with my sister's killer, and if I hadn't been in love with her, I wouldn't have felt the guilt that was consuming me as I leaned over her dead body. And that's when I started to stab her over and over again until I was exhausted. I collapsed, and my mother pulled me off Annie and then we left. I was so angry with her, I ran away. *That's* the truth of what happened, not whatever lies my mother told you in her misguided attempt to protect me. I don't want to be protected. All I want is justice. I delivered it for my sister. Annie is dead, and suffered just as my sister did. Mr. Dettman is dead for using his connections to deny justice, and Mrs. Dettman has now lost everything so she can suffer like my mother did. And now I'm going to be dead soon, so my parents can suffer for their lies and deceit. Everybody gets what they deserve!" He folded his arms, glaring at Vogel. "I'm done talking. I'll sign whatever confession you want. I just want to get this over with."

Vogel leaned back, saying nothing, instead searching the man's eyes. Everything that had just been said finally fit the facts of the case. Arland's mother had tried to cover for him. She had brought the knife, for what purpose he could only guess, though the obvious one was that she had intended to kill Annie herself.

Yet she hadn't.

Arland had taken the knife and killed her once the truth was revealed to him. Vogel had seen it before, where someone was a slave to a recessed part of their mind that turned them into an automaton, their actions beyond their control, usually brought on by some shock to the system. Finding out that the woman he loved, the woman he had just been intimate with, the woman he had planned to run away and spend the rest of his life with, was responsible for the death of his sister, had proven too much.

And with that knife in plain sight, he delivered the justice his sister had never received, no matter how misguided it was. It explained why she had been tied up as she had been, it explained the cold-bloodedness of the slit throat, and how, after watching her bleed out for several minutes before his eyes, it had given him time to regain control, to recognize what he had done, and for the rage and shame to take control, resulting in the emotional frenzy of the multiple stab wounds that had nothing to do with justice or punishment, and everything to do with frustration and anger.

His version of the story also explained why, if his mother were the murderer, he hadn't stopped her. It corroborated Petra Berkner's account that she had cleaned up the apartment, not his mother as she had falsely confessed after he had prompted her. Everything fit the facts of the case, and as far as he was concerned, the case was closed.

Arland Nicklas had murdered Annie Dettman after his mother had informed him of her involvement in his sister's death, and in a dissociative state, had punished her for her perceived crime.

Arland was guilty of murder, his mother was guilty of bringing the murder weapon and handling the situation poorly, both parents were guilty of lying to their son for years, Annie's father was guilty of ordering the death of Corporal Friedel thinking he was protecting his wife, he and his wife Johanna were guilty of forcing a future upon Annie that she was so disgusted by, so terrified of, she had been forced to go behind their backs to find the love she so desperately wanted, to thwart their plans.

Everyone was guilty of something in this case.

Except poor Annie Dettman, who had only wanted to be loved, and thought she had found it in her long lost friend, who had given herself willingly to a man she loved and thought loved her, and whose final moments on God's earth were filled with terror as the man she trusted most in the world, sentenced her to death for a crime she had never committed.

Vogel pictured his daughter, and his eyes burned as he imagined her future in these horrible times, and could only pray that the war would soon be over, his country defeated, and freed from those who would commit atrocities such as what happened this past weekend.

Yet he lived in the real world, and had no doubt there were countless Arland's out there, waiting to be triggered into murdering some other poor innocent.

And though he wouldn't be able to stop them, he wouldn't rest until he brought every single one of them to justice.

Arland slammed his fist on the table. "Well, are you just going to sit there, or are you going to give me my justice?"

Vogel frowned, shaking his head. "You have no idea what justice is. Annie was a child that made a mistake, your parents protected you from the truth so you wouldn't have to suffer like they did, and the Dettmans did what they had to do to protect their daughter from the emotional consequences of her mistake. No court in the land would have convicted her of anything, no matter who her father was.

"You claim everyone is guilty, and that you've now delivered justice. You're a fool. All you've done is murder an innocent girl who loved you, destroyed your own family who never did anything wrong, and forced Mr. Dettman to kill an innocent man because he thought he was protecting his wife for a crime you committed. Other than questionable parenting choices, there is only one guilty party here, and it's you." He leaned forward. "And I promise you this. I'll be there to see you swinging from the end of the hangman's rope, and when you do, you can receive your final judgment, not here in this world gone mad, but before God, where I hope he shows no mercy on your selfish soul."

Vogel rose and stepped out of the room, slamming the door behind him. He entered the crowded observation room and stared at Arland in silence with the others. The misguided murderer's head dropped to the table and his shoulders began to shake with the realization of what he had done, his defiance and self-satisfaction gone.

And the corners of Vogel's lips curled slightly. "Now he gets to spend his remaining days suffering with the knowledge of what he's done."

The Captain slapped him on his back. "Good job, Wolfgang. Why don't you go home and get some rest? You look like shit."

Vogel grunted. "Thanks, Captain, but there's something I have to do first."

"What's that?"

"Go invite my partner to dinner."

THE END

ACKNOWLEDGMENTS

What a joy it is to write something that took me entirely out of this horrible world in which we now live. This book was written during the COVID-19 crisis, a crisis that at the moment shows no signs of ending. With this novel set in 1941 Nazi Germany, there were no parallels to today's problems, however I think I would prefer our current circumstances over what life must have been like living under Nazi rule.

While this novel was an interesting bit of escapism, the research did reveal some fascinating pieces of history of which I wasn't aware. For those with the time, I highly recommend searching the term "Lebensborn" then read up on the Nazi plan to repopulate not only their country, but their "Lebensraum." It is an interesting, though disturbing bit of a troubled past.

And now a little piece of trivia. Check out the name of the shoe factory. Put the first and last names together, then hit Wikipedia for some eye popping history about what is now a major shoe company.

As usual, there are people to thank. My dad for all the research, and, as always, my wife, daughter, my late mother who will always be an angel on my shoulder as I write, as well as my friends for their continued support, and my fantastic proofreading team!

To those who have not already done so, please visit my website at www.jrobertkennedy.com, then sign up for the Insider's Club to be notified of new book releases. Your email address will never be shared or sold.

Thank you once again for reading.